THE MUTINY

OF THE

LAPTWING.

BY

E. HARCOURT BURRAGE.

THE
MUTINY OF THE LAPWING.

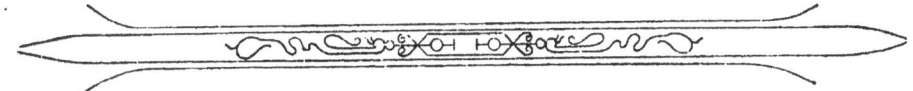

CHAPTER I.

WANTED A CREW—A ROUGH VOLUNTEER—ONE OF A BETTER SORT—
ARTICLES SIGNED.

"WE must get what hands we can, and I can lick 'em into shape when we are out at sea."

Captain Joshua Broadman, of the Lapwing, spoke thus to Mr. Stephen Hartmoor, manager to the great shipping firm of Smith, Pickerell, and Green.

"Getting what we can is risky work," said the manager, dubiously.

"But the Lapwing's bound to sail," urged the captain. She will be expected at the island."

"What an accursed thing this striking is," said the manager, after a pause; "and fancy sailors, of all men, going on that racket."

"I maintain the men generally aint well-treated," replied the captain, "but I don't agree with strikes. It's a fool's game, and only pays one party, and that's those who get them up—leaders, they call 'em."

"Well, leaving all that out, you want to sail, and you can't sail without a crew," said the manager, "so I'll let it be known that there's an opening for free labour. You go on board, and I ll send on the articles to be signed. Having once got the men, don't let 'em go for a moment. Keep 'em on the Lapwing."

"I'll do so. Of course I've Brown and Chipping to help me," replied the captain. "We've got the stores aboard, and as soon as the men are there off we go."

The Lapwing was lying in the South London Docks, as she had been for a week, ready to sail.

But she could get no men, because one of those insensate strikes which are continually convulsing the labour world was on.

The docks were picketted in the usual way, but a few men, with the aid of the police, got through.

Shortly after the captain returned on board one of these men presented himself and offered to sign articles.

He looked like a seaman, yet there was something of the landsman, and not of the better sort, about him.

A stubbly head of hair, with rough whiskers that met under the chin, might have given him a more villainous appearance than his disposition warranted. At least so thought the captain, and without any inquiries worth mentioning the services of the rugged volunteer were accepted.

"And when I've signed," he said, "I'd like to go ashore a bit."

"That is the very thing we want to avoid," replied the captain. "If once the pickets get hold of you, you won't come back again."

"Oh! the pickets won't touch me," was the reply. "If they do may I lose my honoured name o' Dan Ricketts. What's more, I'm going to look up some men for you, and shatter my head-lights if I don't bring 'em to join."

Captain Broadman was very loth to let him go, but Brown, the first mate—a bluff sailor of the old school—coming into the cabin, he was consulted on the matter, and his advice was—"Let him go."

"If he doesn't come back any more," he said, "it isn't of much consequence, but if he really can bring a dozen men it will help us."

So Dan Ricketts was allowed to leave, and within a quarter of an hour of his retiring another volunteer appeared.

The second comer was of different mould, being a young, good-looking fellow, with a head of curly light hair and a retiring, almost timid, bearing.

"And what do you want, my lad?" asked the captain.

"To go to sea, sir," was the reply.

"What for—to get drowned?"

"I think I shall make a sailor if you'll give me a chance."

"So they all think till they try it," said the captain. "Well, what age are you?"

"Eighteen."

"Parents living?"

"No."

"Ever been to sea before?"

"Not for a voyage."

"Then you don't know anything about a seaman's work?"

"Nothing. But I can learn."

"Humph! Apprenticed to anyone?"

"No."

The captain looked at him closely, and thought there was something in the youth to like, but his knowing nothing of seaman's work was the great thing against him.

" It's like taking you for a pleasure trip," Captain Broadman said, "for you see you have everything to learn.   You won't earn your salt first voyage."

" I beg of you to take me," returned the youth. " I will earn not only my salt, but my bread, somehow.   You will find me apt and ready to learn."

" You speak fair, anyway.   What's your name ?"

" Jim Bentley."

" Christened James, I suppose ?"

" Yes."

" Got any trade to your back ?   Do you know anything of carpentering or work of that sort ?"

" I know nothing," replied Jim ; " but, as I tell you, I'm ready to learn."

" What put it into your head to go to sea ?" asked the captain.

" I've thought of it many a day, but I could never see any chance to do so until I heard of this strike."

" Then you thought we'd be glad to have you ?" said the captain, grimly.

" I thought there was a better chance of being taken," replied Jim Bentley.

" How did you get through the pickets ?"

"They let me pass, saying I had better go and help to sink the ship.   I told them I might one day have the chance of saving one."

" And then ?"

" The fellow snapped his fingers under my nose, and I hit him between the eyes.   We had a bit of a fight, and he gave in."

Captain Boardman now noticed for the first time that the clothes of the youth were slightly disordered, and there was a red mark upon his cheek, as if he had been struck there.

"I like your pluck," said the captain, "but it is a dangerous thing to hit one of the pickets."

"Nobody interfered with us," replied Jim. "They said it was a fair fight, and when it was over I came along."

"I'll try you," said the captain. "Here's the articles. Read 'em over before you sign. There will be no going back on 'em. You don't belong to the class we draw our men from, I can see, but it doesn't follow you won't make a good sailor."

Jim looked over the articles, saw nothing in them to object to, and signed.

"You've done it now," said the captain, smiling, "and I hope you will never repent of it."

"And I hope you won't repent of taking me," replied Jim.

CHAPTER II.

DAN RICKETTS KEEPS HIS WORD—JIM'S HAMMOCK—A KNOCK-DOWN BLOW.

R. BROWN took Jim in hand at once, gave him a kit, showed him the forecastle, and told him to choose his place to swing his hammock.

"And, having chosen it," he said, "keep it. Don't let 'em bounce over you in one thing, or you'll have a devil of a life."

As Jim knew nothing about swinging a hammock he was instructed in the art of doing it, and showed such aptitude that he was favoured with a high commendation, rarely bestowed by an old salt upon novices.

Mr. Chipping, the second mate, who had been ashore looking in vain for some men to form a crew, now appeared on board.

He was a tall, lean man, with a saturnine face, and on seeing Jim Bentley busy about some little affair the first mate had set him to do on deck he asked what he was doing there.

"I've joined the ship, sir," replied Jim.

"Joined your grandmother," grumbled Mr. Chipping. "What good do you think you will be?"

"Time will prove that," said Jim, spiritedly.

"We are getting something aboard, Mr. Brown," bawled Chipping to the first mate, who was coming up from below. "Got any babies concealed?"

"You give the young fellow a chance," replied Brown. "But perhaps you've landed a better sort of fish？"

"Not so much as a sprat," replied Chipping, in disgust. "Hallo! what's this? Another row?"

They could hear the roar of voices, hissing and hooting, and knew pretty well what it meant—a contingent of so-called "blacklegs" were endeavouring to force a way into the docks.

"That's a fight—a real one!" said Brown, emphatically, "and, by George! the fellows are making their way up. There they come, through the gates."

About a dozen men in the far distance were seen to rush in, and immediately behind them a line of police was formed to keep out an angry, surging crowd.

After a struggle the police succeeded in forcing

back the mob of strikers, and then the gates were closed.

Coming on, with their clothing torn and faces bruised and bleeding, were a number of about the roughest characters Jim Bentley had ever seen.

At the head of them, with a deep gash under his left eye, where he had been struck with a stick, was Dan Ricketts.

True to his word, he had come back with a number of men to form the crew of the Lapwing.

Her full complement of hands was twenty, but under pressure she could be worked with fourteen.

The number now approaching was twelve—eleven and Dan Ricketts.

It was very clear as they approached that they had all been drinking.   Dan, to put the true state of the case, was pretty well drunk.

"Here we are," he said, as he rolled on board. "Where's the captain?   Let him now tell me that I'm a runaway and a liar."

"Nobody wants to tell you anything of the sort," replied the first mate, whom he addressed, "and on board the Lapwing you will be good enough to moderate your style of address."

"All right, governor, I'll mind," said Ricketts; "but we had to fight our way here, and that's excited me a bit.   Now, mates, come aboard and show yourselves.   There they are—a likely lot. Good seamen, every one."

The appearance of the men introduced with this eulogistic address hardly justified the encomiums bestowed upon them.

They were of mixed races—English, French, Portuguese, Spanish, Swedes, and what not—as rascally a looking lot as one would find in a week's march.

But it seemed, on their being examined, that they knew enough of a seaman's duty to work a ship under orders.

So articles were signed, and it was arranged that the Lapwing should drop down the river the next morning with the ebb-tide—about eleven o'clock.

Meanwhile some good sailors' clothes were served out, and materials for supper, even to the grog, although some of the men would have been better without it.

Jim found himself among a crew that made him heart-sick.

They took very little notice of him at first, but after a time they began to question him much after the style of the captain, only the questions were put in rough form.

He was not, however, molested, and all went well until the time came to turn in.

Jim was the very first to sling his hammock, and having a choice of place he put it up near the door, so as to have as much fresh air as possible.

"Here, youngster, this won't do," said Dan Ricketts, as he came into their quarters. "That's the place I've fixed my mind on."

"But you haven't fixed your hammock," replied Jim, "and the place is as much mine as yours."

"Is it?" said Dan Ricketts, with mock suavity, as he drew out his knife. "Now then, down with it, or I cuts it loose."

"If you touch it," replied Jim, without raising his voice, "I'll knock you down."

Dan Ricketts looked him carefully up and down.

walked round him, and with the air of a critic examined him all over.

The other men, who had come in, looked on grinning. Anything in the way of a row or fight could not but be pleasing to them.

"Now, I wonder who we've got here?" said Dan Ricketts. "Is it the champion light weight or a bantam cock as wants his wings clipped?"

Not being favoured with any reply, he leisurely walked up to the head of the hammock, and, raising his knife, was about to cut it down, when Jim Bentley kept his word.

He hit him on the side of the head with a force that laid him down upon the deck, stunned and helpless.

Having so far maintained his right to the position he had assumed, Jim looked to see how the rest took it.

Very quietly.

They looked at each other with a no-business-of-mine expression in their eyes, and proceeded to sling their own hammocks.

As each man chose the best spot for himself one of the very worst was naturally left for Dan Ricketts.

He did not lie insensible long, being made of the material which takes kindly to hard knocks.

Opening his eyes, he sat up and took a steady look about him. Gradually he took in all the bearings of the case.

"I've been knocked down," he said.

"You have," replied Jim.

"And you did it."

"I did."

"All right," said Dan, rising to his feet. "I'll

talk about it to-morrow. Send I may live if I don't get rum treatment after what I've done for you all."

Growling to himself, he swung his hammock, and, following an example which had been set him by the rest, got into it.

In a few minutes all but Jim were snoring.

He lay awake, thinking of his surroundings—not so much in a sense of fear as of repulsion.

When he settled upon going to sea he did not anticipate being thrown among such a terrible lot as this. He had reason to look forward to the future with dread, but should he shirk it?

"No," he said, with his teeth set close; "it's a bad beginning, but the end may be better and brighter. Anyhow, it can't be worse."

Having accepted this philosophical reflection on the situation he fell asleep.

At daylight he and the men were all aroused by Brown and Chipping and set to work.

Dan Ricketts and his friends, thanks to the drinking of the day before, were in a very bleareyed, shaky condition.

They worked in a dogged, silent way, taking no notice of anything or of each other, but just getting through their tasks as they were ordered.

A Frenchman named Morbeau was told off as cook, and he prepared the morning meal of porridge in a satisfactory manner.

They had it by way of a treat, for when at sea dry biscuit and a decoction called cocoa would be supplied in its place.

By noon they were going steadily down the Thames with the tide and a favourable wind, and when night came they were fairly out in the Channel.

CHAPTER III.

A FATAL NUMBER — THREATS — A MUTINY AND A STORM.

ITH thirteen men for a crew you can't have any luck on board," said Dan Ricketts. "Look at the head-winds we've had since we passed Maderia, and now here's a blessed calm upon us—a thing you don't get in this latitude once in ten years."

When men have a certain hat to hang up they never fail to find some sort of peg to hang it on.

Dan Ricketts had learnt to hate Jim Bentley with his whole heart, and so he fixed upon him as being the thirteenth man, who was the cause of all the weather trouble with which the Lapwing had been afflicted.

Everyone, officers included, felt that the vessel was out of luck, for she had had little but adverse winds since she started.

"It looks as if we'd got a Jonah aboard," said the captain, in Dan Rickett's hearing, and then that astute personage hit upon the thirteenth-man idea.

He had also another idea in his head, and that was the Lapwing was laden with treasure of some sort.

Down in the hold there were sundry boxes, which the captain and first mate inspected every few days with great care, to see if they had been tampered with, as it was supposed.

Furthermore, the destination of the Lapwing was

HASTILY BREAKING OFF A BRANCH JIM RUSHED TO THE RESCUE OF THE CAPTAIN.

not known. The men had simply signed for a six months' voyage—"out and home."

Ricketts and his friends were often in close conversation when Jim was engaged in his duties out of hearing.

The life of the young fellow who is to be our hero was not what he expected, but he held his own with the rough rascals who formed the crew.

That knock-down blow which he gave Dan Ricketts was an excellent introduction to them. The only thing they could appreciate was brute force.

They got it into their heads that he was a scientific boxer, and they had no higher ideal of the excellence of man, so they left him alone.

He, on his part, did his duty, talking no more to the crew than was absolutely necessary, and spending his leisure time reading books which Mr. Brown, the first mate, lent him.

Thus matters were when the Lapwing was becalmed about twenty miles south of the Cape.

For three days not a breath of wind had fluttered the canvas that hung idly against the mast.

The sailors murmured, much louder than they would have done if they had not some motive beyond grumbling about the weather.

"If we get rid of that young 'un," said Ricketts, "we can do as we please. Take our own time, lads, and grab the yellow boys is the word."

"How do you know they are yellow boys?" asked Morbeau, the cook.

"What should they be?" replied Ricketts. "Don't you see how they are allers going down to look at the cases? It's my opinion that we are bound for India with some money for a rajah chap."

The idea took root.

It worked upon them until the deadly gold-hunger laid hold of them, but they were sufficiently under the control of Dan Ricketts to proceed warily.

Dan Ricketts wanted to get up a quarrel with the captain, and after thinking the matter over he decided on objecting to the crew being thirteen in number.

Accordingly on the afternoon of the third day of the calm he approached the captain, who was pacing slowly up and down the deck.

"Beg pardon, captain," he said, touching his cap, "but may I make so bold as to speak to you?"

"Well, what do you want?" asked the captain, curtly. Ricketts was no favourite with him.

"It's about the bad luck as the Lapwing's had."

"Yes?"

"There's a cause for it, in course, sir, and we have come to the conclusion that it's the crew being thirteen in number as has done it."

"Yes?"

"And we've settled that one's got to be sent about his business."

"How?"

"Anyhow. If a ship laden with a big cargo is labouring in a storm, what's done, sir? Why, she's lightened of a part of that 'ere cargo."

"Very well, Ricketts; you can easily lighten the Lapwing," said the captain, with a twinkle of the eye.

"You give me leave, sir?" exclaimed Ricketts.

"You don't want leave to jump overboard, do you, man?"

"Me, sir?" gasped Ricketts, aghast. "Me, sir, go overboard? What for, sir?"

"To make the number of the crew even, of course," answered the captain.

"That wouldn't do it," said Ricketts, after a dismayed pause. "It aint me, or any as come with me, as is the wrong 'un. We are twelve good men and true, and are right enough. It's that young Bentley as puts everything wrong."

"Indeed!" returned the captain, drily. "For a wrong one he does his work remarkably well. Although only a short time at sea, he's as good a seaman as half of you, and more willing than all of you put together. Go back to your duty, and don't talk nonsense about thirteen being unlucky."

Dan Ricketts swung himself round, and was walking sullenly away when the captain called him back.

"I'll thank you to behave civilly to me," he said. "Touch your cap, or I'll throw you overboard myself."

Ricketts touched his cap and slouched off to the forecastle, where, having nothing else to do, he threw himself down, and lay like some ill-tempered beast upon the deck.

"I'll do it to-night," he growled, "and I'll lighten the Lapwing of more than one of them."

The darkness came in due course, and the captain, with his two mates, were in the former's cabin, studying the barometer.

It had stood very high during the calm, but it now showed the slightest possible tendency to fall.

"It may go down with a rush about midnight," he said, "and I think we had better have the stern sails set. A close watch must be kept till the morning."

"It's my watch to-night," said Mr. Brown.

He cast another look at the barometer. Yes, it was clearly falling, and a breeze of some sort might soon be expected.

He had just left the cabin and put one foot on the companion when Jim Bentley came tumbling down.

"Look to yourself!" he said. "The crew are in open mutiny."

His words were heard by the captain and second mate, both of whom rushed out of the cabin.

"What's that I hear?" cried the captain.

Jim repeated what he had said.

"They have armed themselves with knives and belaying pins," he added, "and they intend to kill us all."

"Steady, my lads," said Captain Broadman. "Chipping, there are revolvers in my chest—loaded. Hand 'em out—I'll mutiny 'em!"

"Hallo! you down there," cried Dan Ricketts from above.

"What's the matter?" asked the captain.

"Come up at once; somebody's taken ill."

"Very well," answered the captain, "I'll bring him a pill. Ready, Chipping?"

"Here you are, sir."

A revolver each was hastily handed around, and the captain, with a determined growl, headed the way upstairs.

Dan Ricketts had given way to another of the men, and the captain shot him right away, without a query or a word of expostulation.

The effect upon the mutineers was like that of a shock from a tremendously powerful galvanic battery.

They leaped back and spread all over the deck.

Up went the captain, followed by the two mates and Jim. One glance was sent aloft, and it was at once seen that two perils were to be faced.

High overhead, across the face of the moon, a rack was flying like marsh mists in a gale.

"Up and reef the sails, you dogs, one and all!" roared the captain.

The men, instead of obeying, ran aft and hid themselves behind a rough barricade of barrels and boxes.

As they disappeared the captain fired again, and a howl of anguish escaped from one of the men.

He was seen to fall and lie on his side, where he lay groaning.

"I'll teach you to mutiny, you villains!" said the captain. "D'ye hear? Go aloft and do your duty."

"And get shot for our trouble," replied Dan Ricketts. "Not if we knows it, until you chucks them popping irons on the deck."

Lower and lower sank the rack in the sky. The captain cast an anxious look aloft.

"We haven't five minutes," he said, "and coming so suddenly it will be a cyclone."

As he spoke a noise was heard aft, and, turning their eyes in that direction, the startled officers saw a white line coming over the sea towards them.

"Lord have mercy upon us!" ejaculated the captain.

With a force that was new in the experience of Jim Bentley the first rush of the wind-storm broke on the ship.

Luckily it struck her clean aft, or she must have heeled over and gone down.

As it was she was lifted a bit, so that her bow nearly plunged under the sea, and then raced forward.

The captain sprang to the helm.

With a motion of his arm—words could not have

been heard—he signified his desire that Jim should stand by and give him a hand in case it was needed.

Jim had to battle his way to the captain's side, but when there he laid hold of the wheel, and stood ready to respond to any movement he might make.

On sped the Lapwing.

And now the rack became a dense cloud, obscuring all things.

On, on, with lightning speed, dashed the doomed vessel, over waves that suddenly rose like mountains in its path, and then through deep valleys of seething waters.

Keeping a look-out under the circumstances would have been useless. The men on board did not stir.

So they carried on—for an hour or more, it may be —and then the Lapwing suddenly stopped.

She had struck!

Jim had no time to think of what had happened.

The tremendous shock sent him clean over the vessel's side into the boiling sea.

‘   .   .   .   .   .   .

When he opened his eyes again Jim saw a blue, clear sky above his head. A gentle breeze fanned his brow.

He took his time to think out what had happened, and then recalled it all.

He sat up and looked around him.

At his feet, a hundred yards or so away, was the comparatively quiet sea.

But whot is this he sees?

Captain Broadman lying senseless or dead upon the shore, and Dan Ricketts stealing towards him with his knife between his teeth.

Jim instinctively felt for his revolver.

It was gone.

In an agony he cast his eyes about him for a weapon wherewith to go to the aid of the captain.

There was none, and the only possible means of obtaining one was by tearing a branch from a tree near him.

He darted towards it, and, hastily breaking off the end of a lower limb, rushed to the rescue of the captain, just as Dan Ricketts threw himself with all his force upon him.

Then, for the first time, Jim saw that the captain's eyes were wide open.

He was alive.

CHAPTER IV

A GALLANT RESCUE—THE OLD SHIP—A DINNER ON BOARD.

WHETHER Captain Broadman was insensible when Dan Ricketts pounced upon him, or only lying in a semi-dazed state, was uncertain, but the moment the ruffian fastened his hand upon his throat he appeared to fully realise the peril of his position.

He began to struggle violently, which occupied the attention of Ricketts, who otherwise must have clearly seen Jim Bentley bearing down upon him.

"Ah! you tyrannical warmint," he said to the captain, "going and doing your best to get honest people drowned. I'll settle yer!"

But this could not be done immediately, for both his hands were required to keep down the gallant old seaman, and the knife which Ricketts was obliged to hold between his teeth was entirely useless.

A blow that would have fractured a skull of ordinary density served only to make him see a star or two and apprise him of the arrival of a third party on the scene.

Looking up, he saw Jim in the act of striking him again, and letting go of the captain's throat he sprang to his feet.

"Leave off, you cub!" he cried. "What yer mean by laying 'bout you in that style?"

Jim felt as weak as a rat, but keeping up a show of strength and agility he made a rush at the ruffian, who, muttering curses, beat a rapid retreat, running along the shore and vanishing behind a projecting portion of the cliff.

"Well done, and timely done, my lad," said the captain, heartily. "But for you I was food for the wild beasts this time, sure. Where did you hail from?"

Jim explained that he had only just recovered consciousness, and had but a very imperfect idea of how he got ashore.

"You came with the rest of us," replied the captain, grimly, "anyhow and nohow—that is, if the rest of 'em *are* ashore."

"You haven't seen them, then?" inquired Jim.

"Not a soul. That skunk Ricketts is the only one I've set eyes on till I saw you. Maybe *he's* alone."

The captain stood up stiffly and gave his knee-joints a rubbing, of which they seemed to be in sore need.

Meanwhile Jim took a look about him, and with joy espied the hull of a vessel—which no doubt was the Lapwing—lying on the shore about a mile and a half up the coast.

He pointed it out to the captain, who, after a close survey, said he thought it was his vessel, but couldn't be sure, as the hurricane had made a clean shave of masts and rigging.

The hull was almost as bare as an unfitted vessel in the docks.

"But we can go and see, my lad," he said, "for if it is the Lapwing she's got stores aboard, and we sha'n't starve."

As she lay in the opposite direction to that taken by Dan Ricketts there was no fear of a second encounter with him.

A sandy beach, left by a receding tide, enabled them to perform the journey with tolerable ease, although both felt it advisable to rest once or twice on the way.

"It's a stiff knocking about we've had, my lad," said the captain, "but it'll wear off in a day or so. No bones broken."

On reaching the Lapwing, which the wreck turned out to be, the prospect of getting on board did not at first seem a very hopeful one.

There was positively only one short piece of rope dangling over the side, and that was out of reach.

"But I think I can hoist you up," said the captain, "and if you lay hold and climb you can get something for me to mount by."

Jim was light and the captain was naturally strong, so up he went, and after a short delay a ship's ladder was dropped over the side.

Captain Broadman ascended and joined Jim on deck.

The Lapwing—having by the force with which she had been driven on the shore got deepish into the sand, and a few boulders of rock being fortuitously placed so as to act as supports—lay upon an almost even keel.

It was as easy to get about her as it had been at sea during calm weather.

Nothing that had been moveable or could be torn away by the wind had been left on the deck.

Of the masts only the most pitiful stumps remained, and every vestige of canvas and rigging had disappeared.

From the deck they looked around, and saw that they had been cast upon a beautiful shore.

As it could not possibly be the mainland of a continent, so the captain said, it was therefore an island, and south of Madagascar.

There were high cliffs in one direction, and in the other a splendid beach. As far as they could see of the interior it was luxuriously wooded.

The only signs of life were the birds and insects in the air. Nothing human was in sight.

The captain went below to his cabin and brought up his telescope, with which he carefully scanned the island.

"I see nothing of the others," he said, "neither living or dead, and I reckon that you and I and that skunk Ricketts are the only survivors."

"It was a most merciful escape," replied Jim. "I suppose a vessel will soon come this way and take us off."

"Can't say, my lad," replied the captain. "I reckon we are out of the course of *all* vessels, but I'll take the bearings directly and make sure. Meanwhile I think you and I had better have something to eat and drink. Haul up that ladder and clear away the bit o' rope. That'll keep out visitors who might be disposed to be more free than welcome."

Jim hauled the ladder in and cut away the piece of rope as directed. Then he went below to assist with the dinner or breakfast, or whatever they chose to call it.

A visit to the store-room gave them the materials for a hearty meal—preserved beef, biscuits, bottled fruit, and claret—which were laid out in the captain's cabin.

"To-day we'll have wine," said the captain, "and to-morrow tea, in case we should have to husband the stimulant. There's about six dozen of the former and a few kegs of whisky and rum on board—that's all."

"But surely that will be enough until we are rescued," said Jim, with a smile.

"My lad," replied the captain, "we may be here for years—perhaps for the rest of our days. There isn't, as far as I can see, the least sign of civilised man having put foot on this island before."

"But there may be natives," suggested Jim.

"I pray to Heaven there isn't," answered the captain, as he raised his glass of wine, "for they are sure to be both bloodthirsty and cruel. However, we'll wait till they come—and here's good luck to us and a speedy rescue."

CHAPTER V.

A PLEASANT HOUR—DAN RICKETTS IS CALLED UP— HE GETS A WARNING.

AFTER dinner the captain routed out two big Japanese umbrellas, with small spikes in their handles, which he said he had often used before.

"When on the island—THE island," he said, "of which you will hear more if ever we are taken off from here, we'll carry 'em about with us everywhere—opening 'em and sticking 'em in the soft ground when we lie down for a cooler."

He planted them on deck close to the side of the vessel nearest the sea, so that they could put their backs against the bulwarks.

Then he brought out a handful of cigars he had taken from a locker below and offered one to Jim.

"Cigars to-day," he said, "and one every Sunday until further notice. Tobacco for the rest of the week in moderation."

Matches had been obtained from the same source, and, having lighted their cigars, Captain Broadman sat for awhile thinking deeply.

Jim did not interrupt his thoughts, for he was thinking too—not only of his present predicament, but of many things in the old country, and of people who by this time would be wondering where he was.

Presently the voice of the captain was heard.

"Have a quiet glance round, lad," he said, "just to see nobody's hanging round the vessel, as I don't want any listeners to what I have to say."

Jim had a careful look about, but, as before, there was no sign of a human being. Returning to his place he sat down beside the captain.

"In the first place, my lad," he said, "I'll start with this. It is no longer captain and seaman, but two friends who are talking together. You don't belong to the Dan Ricketts' school. If you did you would be at one end of the vessel and me at the other, lonely as we are, for you can't be free with some men."

"I am sure I am much obliged to you," said Jim, "and if you think it necessary I can go back to my old position at any time."

"There'll never be any necessity, my lad. As for the future—why, I look to see you in a very different position, and you shall be if I have the ruling of it. Now we come to the cargo we have on board. What do you think it is?"

"Gold," promptly answered Jim.

"Wrong," chuckled the captain. "Miles out. It's not specie of any sort, or jewels, or anything, but just *dynamite*."

Jim started, and stared at the captain with an expression of face that made the grim seaman chuckle again.

"Don't be afraid of it," he said; "it's harmless enough at present, if let alone."

"I am not afraid," returned Jim, "but I must confess that I felt startled when you named it."

"Now I daresay you wonder what it was for," said the captain, with a knowing cock of his eye.

"Well, I should like to know, of course," confessed Jim.

"And if I say I would rather you did not know for the present?"

"Then I shall be content to wait."

"Well spoken, my lad. If we never get off here it will be better you did not know, for it would make you unhappy; but if ever we get away *you shall be one of us*, and there's my hand on it."

He shook hands with Jim, took another puff at his cigar, and resumed—

"Now we come to home matters—that is, matters here. First of all we must live on the Lapwing, and never go far away from her until we are sure there's only that Dan Ricketts on the island. We'll rig up an awning on deck, for there's lots of extra canvas below, and we'll live there day and night, bar stormy weather."

"Is there anything in the hold but dynamite?"

"Yes, and I'm coming to that," replied the captain. "There's a lot of arms and ammunition for the use of those I hope you'll be friends with by and bye. But some of it had better be got up for our own use. There's rifles and fowling-pieces and cutlasses there, but for the present we will only take what we want for ourselves."

Having opened the hold, he and Jim descended, and by the aid of the daylight admitted Jim saw that the place was pretty well filled with boxes, so packed and guarded by wooden fastenings that shifting, even in the most violent storm, was impossible.

The captain selected a particular case, and, assisted by Jim, got it on deck.

THEN CAME THE REPORT OF A RIFLE—AND DAN RICKETTS LET GO HIS HOLD.

On carefully opening it half a dozen weapons, four of which were in a disjointed condition, were disclosed.

These were fowling-pieces and rifles; the other weapons were revolvers.

Several boxes of cartridges were fitted into the intermediate spaces.

"These guns," said the captain, "can be put together this way. You simply insert the barrel into the stock, turn the lever, and then it is in working order. Number one box contains bullet-cartridges, number two shot-cartridges, and number three those for the revolvers.

"There are fifty cases like this below, each intended for the use of two men," added the captain. "Fill your revolver and wear it. The guns can be kept in my cabin until wanted."

The hold was closed up again and securely locked, as it had hitherto been.

The next step was to arrange the aft deck for living purposes.

It was now near noon, and while Jim was engaged in getting up from the ship's store-room the needed materials the captain fetched up his sextant and carefully adjusted it.

A chronometer in its case in the cabin had gone on faithfully recording the flight of time, and it indicated the approach of noon.

High overhead hung the sun, shining down with a power that truly was enough to bake the brain-pan of a man.

But Jim went on with his work until the captain called a halt. He had taken his observations, and found they were about a hundred miles south of Madagascar.

" It's an island, and a lone one," he said. " There's a dot for it on some maps, but I don't think it's ever been named. My lad, we've got here, and we've come to stay."

He carefully replaced the sextant, carried it below, and returned to the deck, where he paced to and fro for awhile.

Jim went on with his work, stretching a low awning aft. He was a useful fellow, with a knack of turning his hand to anything, and had the gift of always being interested in what he was doing.

In the midst of an absorbing mental calculation he was startled by a shout—

" Ricketts, ahoy !"

Captain Broadman had lungs that would have served a grampus for double extra blowing-power, and his voice echoed along the shore.

Jim looked up, and saw Ricketts on a cliff about two hundred yards away, in the attitude of a man who is doubtful whether he ought to advance or retreat.

" Ricketts, ahoy !" shouted the captain again.

The cry was accompanied by a beckoning of the hand, which Ricketts thought proper to obey.

But he came along very slowly, and when within fifty yards halted.

" Come nearer," cried the captain ; " nobody is going to hurt you."

But Ricketts was not sure of that. He had good reason to know that the captain was not particularly desirous of his company, and might possibly be meditating some disagreeable move.

" Come nearer still, so that I need not shout," said the captain.

Ricketts crept up another few yards, and the captain was satisfied.

"Are you hungry?" he asked.

"Well, I aint had anything to eat yet," growled Ricketts.

"Stop a minute and I'll get you a biscuit," said the captain.

He got him two, which he deftly shied in the direction of the expectant Ricketts.

"That's all you'll get to-day," continued the captain, "and just you listen to me. You see that bit o' cliff that looks like a big flat stone?"

"Yes, I sees it," growled Ricketts.

"Well, that's your boundary-line," said the captain. "You keep on the tother side o' that, or, by the lord, I'll put a bullet through you."

"I aint likely to come nigh," said Ricketts. "There aint anything to eat on the island as I can see. The trees is a sort o' pine, and there's no shellfish, it appears."

"Look here, Ricketts," said Captain Broadman, "you behaved badly to me. You mutinied and then tried to murder me. But I'm going to give you a chance for your life. You shall have a bag o' biscuit left on the cliff to-morrow, and while that lasts you are all right. After that you must shift for yourself. Now clear off, and don't let me see so much as the tip o' your nose again to-day."

"But, captain, have some marcy on a man," pleaded Ricketts. "I'm sorry for what I done, in course, and there's two to one of you."

"Clear off," said the captain. "I won't be bothered with you. Be smart, I'm not a bad shot."

He took out his revolver as if about to shoot, and Ricketts, not caring to trust himself within range, wheeled round and trotted off, looking back now and again to see that no mischief was intended him.

CHAPTER VI.

DAN RICKETTS' DASTARD ATTEMPT—A STARTLING
FALL—VOICES OF THE NIGHT.

T a very early hour the two men cast into each other's society on an equal footing under such strange circumstances were glad to lie down and seek repose.

As they had no means of slinging hammocks they made up a rough kind of bed on the hard deck, and, after carefully scanning the prospect with the aid of a night-glass and the moon, went fearlessly to sleep.

Believing Dan Ricketts to be the only other living person within hail, they had no fear of him.

Jim, in particular, was not troubled about his old foe, whom he had tested and proved to be a cur.

Whether Dan was alone or not they were undisturbed, and at sunrise both were up and stirring.

As promised, the captain filled a bag with biscuit, and would have proceeded with it to the top of the cliff but for Jim insisting on taking that office upon himself.

"Keep a sharp look-out for him," said the captain at starting; "he's a leary customer."

Jim, laughing and saying he was not afraid of him, shouldered the bag and went down the ladder, previously lowered for the purpose.

The route he had to take lay along the lower ground and by a somewhat roundabout way to the appointed spot.   It was possible from the deck of the Lapwing to keep watch over him nearly the entire distance.

Ere he had been long gone a feeling of uneasiness tole over the captain.

He knew nothing whatever about the encounter between Jim and Ricketts at an earlier stage of their acquaintance, in which the latter had been signally worsted, and he had a fear that if Dan Ricketts had the temerity to lie in wait for the youth he might bring about a balance of accounts in his favour.

So he watched the progress of Jim until he had reached his destination, and it was with a sigh of relief he saw him deposit the bag and walk slowly back on the edge of the cliff.

From the small figure in the distance his eye traversed to the country round, and away, about half a mile on the right, he saw another figure bearing down towards Jim.

Not openly, but by stealth, seizing every natural obstacle to cover his approach.   It was Dan Ricketts, without a doubt.

Trembling with rage, Captain Boardman dived down into his cabin, and speedily returned with a rifle in his hand.

Descending the vessel's side, he ran along the beach, hoping, by keeping to the lower ground, to speedily attract Jim's attention, and so warn him of his danger.

Jim, on his part, was sauntering along in a dreamy mood, not looking inland or behind him, but seaward.

He did not even see the captain until he heard him shouting.

Looking down, he saw him gesticulating violently, but his actions were incomprehensible and his voice was indistinct. What was it he wanted?

A sound of footsteps near him caused Jim to turn round just in time to perceive Dan Ricketts as he sprang upon him.

" Now, my lad!" he hissed, " I've got you, and over you go."

IIe had taken Jim so far by surprise that he forced him down upon his knees, on the edge of the cliff.

One leg, indeed, hung over, and the power of resistance was almost taken away from him.

All he could do was to hold on tightly to his foe, and that he did right manfully.

" Let go, will you?" roared Dan.

" No, you villain." replied Jim. " If I fall you will go with me."

It was almost a sheer fall of a hundred feet he was threatened with—apparently certain death—and it would hardly compensate him to know that Dan Ricketts accompanied him.

Half a dozen times they swung to and fro, and the result of the struggle was still undecided. Then came the report of a rifle, and Dan Ricketts let go his hold.

At the same moment Jim also slackened his grasp, with the result that he went over the edge of the cliff.

Scrambling and clutching at every little projection, he slid down with inconceivable velocity until he encountered a protuberance, on which he stuck.

There he rested for an instant ere it broke away, and down he went again—not so fast as before, but still fast enough to give him an idea of the end of the journey being very unpleasant.

He continued his rapid descent until he found his progress stopped by something soft, with which he went rolling over and over for a dozen yards or so, and then lay still.

"Saved, my lad!" he heard the captain gasp, and then he knew that the soft object was the somewhat portly form of that cheery sailor.

It was fully a minute ere he could sit up and make reply, tendering his thanks for the help so opportunely rendered him.

"I caught you just as you would have come thump on the sands," said the captain, exultingly. "Not broke anything, I hope. Can you stand up?"

"Oh! yes," replied Jim, suiting the action to the reply.

"Feel your arms and legs—shake 'em."

"It's more the scare I feel," said Jim. "By Jingo! what a rush. I thought I had fallen half a mile at least."

The captain had lain down his rifle to go to his help.

Picking it up, he opened the chamber, took out the discharged cartridge, and put in a fresh one.

"I hope I dropped him," he said, looking up. "I know I hit him."

"He staggered back," replied Jim, "but I don't think you have killed him."

"Perhaps you didn't wait to see."

"I did *not*," replied Jim, laughing.

As he had now fairly well recovered from his fall they set out for the ship again.

While they were under the cliff they could not see who was above, but having reached the deck of the Lapwing they looked in the direction of the cliff. Dan Ricketts was not there.

The captain got his powerful glass and surveyed all the places within range, but could find no trace of the villain.

After this experience Captain Boardman decided it would be advisable for them to have a cutlass each, and he foraged out a pair of the good old school—serviceable weapons, which would stand as much chopping and knocking about as a hand-saw.

Jim was not averse to wearing such a thing. It rather suited his fancy. The captain gave him a preliminary lesson in the use of it.

"Old sailors are right," he said; "there's nothing like it. It's done more good, manly work than will ever be got out of big guns."

All that day they were busy perfecting their domestic arrangements and laying their plans for the future.

It would be unendurable to be ever confined to the ship, watching over their "home," so a pair of grappling-irons was fixed to the ship's ladder, and under the lee of a cliff they dug a hiding-place for it.

A simple hole that could be neatly stopped up sufficed.

These and many other things into which we need not go into detail were done, and so the second day came to an end.

The next thing to be thought of was the rigging of a jury-mast on which to fly a signal of distress in "case a vessel came that way."

"But if it does I'm afraid it will come as ours did—against the will of those on board," said the captain. "Anyway, it's as well to be prepared."

It was strange that up to that time not a single

body had been cast on shore, but there was no reasonable hope of any other survivors being on the island.

And yet that night Jim happened to lie awake, and was sure he heard voices near the Lapwing.

There was a gentle breeze blowing at the time, and the sounds were such as one might hear from persons eagerly discussing some knotty question.

But it was by the tone he had to judge. The precise nature of the words he could not hear.

The moon was shining with exceptional brilliancy, as he could see from under the awning. If anybody was at hand surely they could be easily seen.

The captain was quietly sleeping, and Jim thought it would be better not to disturb him. Rising with great caution, he crept out upon the deck, where he crouched awhile, listening.

Undoubtedly it was human voices he heard.

There was the change of tone, the rise and fall, the distinction between one word and the other, and yet nothing he could understand.

Then he tried to locate the sound, but here again he failed.

First it seemed on one side of the vessel, then the other. After that he was nearly sure the speakers were close under the bows.

Finally he crept cautiously to the side, and, raising his head peered over.

The brilliant moonlight would have revealed any living thing a quarter the size of a man, but there was nobody in sight.

In vain he looked here and there, this side and that. He could find naught to account for the sounds, which, strange to say, the moment he looked

Puzzled, he returned to his sleeping-place, and lay there listening. But the sounds were heard no more, and the breeze fell too, so that the almost oppressive silence of a tropical night was on all things around.

The sea, which had sunk nearly to a calm, lazily rolled itself upon the shore, and the slight swish, swish of the succeeding waves only served to make the general quietude more impressive.

It told upon the listener in due time, and the insidious comforter of the night stole upon him once more, wrapping him in a dreamless slumber.

He heard nothing until the voice of the captain sounded in his ears.

"My lad, what makes you sleep so heavy this morning? The sun's been here an hour."

Jim sprang up, and saw that the captain had risen some time ago.

A fire in the galley stove was burning, and he had already prepared coffee.

"When you've calmed down a bit," he said, "I've something to tell you."

Jim looked at his face, and saw it was very grave. But he forebore to question him.

The modest breakfast was soon disposed of, and as Jim was clearing it away the captain observed—

"Did you sleep all right, my lad?"

"No," replied Jim; "I was awake for a good two hours."

"How's that?"

"I thought I heard somebody talking, and I got up to see."

"And you saw nobody?"

"No."

"For all that, my lad, there were men hanging

round the ship last night. If you will look over at
the sand you will see footsteps that are neither mine
nor yours."

Jim did as he was told, and saw a number of
imprints which had not been there the night
before.

Some were of booted feet, but others were naked.

It was not easy to get at the number of the
visitors, for they had walked to and fro, crossing
and recrossing each other.

"What do you make of it?" asked the captain.

"That there are other people on the island,"
replied Jim, quietly, "and they can't be friends, or
they wouldn't come sneaking round in this way—
that's all."

"And enough, too, by my stars," said the captain.
"It strikes me, my lad, that we've got rough times
ahead of us."

––––––

CHAPTER VII.

THE MYSTERY UNEXPLAINED—A NIGHT WATCH—VOICES AGAIN AND A STRANGE LAUGH.

WHO were the mysterious visitants, and from
whence did they come?

Up to that night there had been no sign
of any person being saved beyond themselves and Dan Ricketts, but the evidence that
others were alive on the island was indisputable.

All that day the old captain and Jim discussed
the question, and found no answer to it.

Another matter now attracted the attention of the
captain.

During their first day on board, the tide, when it

came in, just washed its way round the vessel and then retired.

On the second day it seemed to him as if the water rose higher.

Whatever hope may have arisen in his mind from this, he at first thought of keeping it to himself, but eventually he confided it to Jim.

It was in the afternoon of the day—they did not dare to leave the ship until they knew what possible foes they might have to contend with—and Jim was clearing up the remnants of a late dinner, when the captain suddenly smacked his thigh and exclaimed—

"It might come about, and that would be a rare bit o' luck."

Jim looked up inquiringly, and the captain, meeting his eye, proceeded to explain.

"I think the season for high tides—or spring tides, as they are generally called—is coming on us here, and if we could get an extra one I think *the old hulk would float*."

Jim's startled face showed how portentous these words were to him, and the captain hastened to check an overflow of hope.

"We can't be certain of it," he said, "but if it should be so we ought to have something rigged up so as to take us off the shore. Ever so small a bit of canvas would be helpful. A topmast forrard would do it if the wind were favourable."

"It's a chance, certainly," agreed Jim, breathlessly, "and we had better put up the mast at once."

"Steady, my lad—no hurry; we've got to wait at least a week for that tide, and we shall have to stand a siege before then, perhaps. Let us prepare for it."

JIM CUT AND SLASHED UNTIL DAN RICKETS CROUCHED DOWN.

The first thing he did was to get up two other cases of firearms, and, having loaded them, they were hidden away in various parts of the deck, so as to be got at whenever wanted.

"We can't be all over the ship at once," said the captain, "so to have weapons and ammunition in every quarter will save time."

The next thing he brought up—and he would not allow Jim to touch it—was a small wooden box, which he handled with exceeding care.

On opening it with his pocket-knife, round the blade of which he wrapped his handkerchief, he disclosed a number of metal cases about the size and half the length of a candle for carriage lamps.

"Guess what these are," he said.

"I should say they were explosives of some sort," replied Jim.

"Right—dynamite cartridges. Now, in one of these there is power enough to kill twenty men, but I don't want to use them except as a last resource. I don't like things of this pattern, but if there's numbers to prevail against one mustn't be too squeamish."

The cartridges were also hidden away, and to save them from any possible concussion they were thickly wrapped in pieces of cloth and rag.

"A good hard knock is all they want," said the captain, "and then they're off."

Jim looked at them somewhat askance, and at any other time would rather have had them farther off, but the possibility of their being needed was too apparent.

The necessity of their keeping watch in turn had come about, and the captain took first watch that night.

The moon rose late, and for an hour after sunset it was pretty dark. The stars shone out, it is true, but there was a mistiness about them which was very unusual. The captain said it foreboded rain.

"It'll start slowly," he asserted, "but it will come down quick eventually—like a monsoon."

When Jim, who had been busy all day, laid down he soon fell asleep, and Captain Broadman, having removed his shoes, went softly about the deck, listening here and there.

He wanted to hear those voices, as Jim had heard them, and see if he could not fathom the mystery.

He waited for half an hour, and heard nothing. Then something like a distant muffled shout fell upon his ear.

Cautiously he listened over the side, but heard nothing more for a few minutes; then an almost continuous murmuring was heard.

"Human, certainly," he muttered; "but it's like men speaking with their mouths full."

It seemed so near and yet so far away, and he was certain it was not close under the ship.

"I'll wake Jim," he said, "and get at it."

Waking Jim was not so easy, for when a youth has laboured all day in the open air his sleep is generally sound, and two medium shakes failed to rouse him.

"I'll risk it alone," muttered the captain.

Having fixed the grappling-irons of the ladder, he lowered it, and, first taking the precaution to see that he had his pistols handy and in order, he slowly descended to the sands below.

Although very dark, he had good eyes, and a steady look round showed him that nobody was about—or, at least, not moving.

At present all was still, but in the hope that he would hear the voices again he listened, crouching down in the deeper shadow of the vessel.

Presently he heard them again, apparently not far away, and he thought he could recognise the voice of Dan Ricketts.

But where was the man?

All sailors are superstitious, and the possibility of the man having died and come back to haunt him flashed upon the captain.

Perhaps he had wounded him that day, and he had crept like some beast into the bush to die.

"Lord forgive me if it is so!" he said, wiping his brow. "All I did was to save the lad."

Just then, as if in mockery of him, a "Ha! ha!" fell upon his ears.

It sounded so close to him that he started up and whipped out a revolver.

But there was nobody near him.

The moon was above the horizon now, and its light was sufficient to have clearly revealed any human form within a hundred yards, but he could see nobody.

Really alarmed, the captain beat a retreat and scrambled up the ladder, which he drew after him and mechanically coiled upon the deck.

Then he sat down, and dabbed his forehead with his handkerchief, to wipe away the dew of superstitious fear.

"We're haunted—haunted. Lord help us! Life on this island aint worth living now."

Then the footmarks they had seen outside and round the vessel came back to his memory.

"Haunted be hanged!" he growled. "It's that Ricketts playing some game on us to skeer us away.

He must be a natural to think that I'll budge an inch."

When it came to Jim's turn to watch, which he awoke for as if he had been conscious of the time in his sleep, the captain simply said—

"Keep a good look-out, my lad, and don't be afraid of anything you hear. If you see anything shoot it."

Then he laid down, and in his turn fell asleep.

CHAPTER VIII.

THE SURVIVORS OF THE WRECK—DAN RICKETTS HAS A PLAN.

HE spot where the Lapwing had been wrecked was near the point of the island, which was like the form of a slim-built boat.

This fact was not apparent from the deck of the vessel, as it was hidden by a high range of cliffs, which effectually shut out a stretch of land beyond it.

In reality there was nothing but the sea and the horizon to be seen from the wreck.

Now the reader has to imagine himself transported to the other side of this part of the island, not more than half a mile from where the wreck lay, and there, seated at the mouth of a cave, were four men.

They were Dan Ricketts, Morbeau the cook, and two other men named Dribble and Smitch.

Close by was the remnant of another wreck, but not a modern one. By the look of it it might have lain there nearly a century.

It was that of an old French man-of-war, and it lay upon its side with the deck towards the cliff.

In addition to the cave by which the men sat there were many others along the shore. The place was honeycombed with them, great and small.

The work the men were engaged upon was that of cleaning up and sharpening some old rusty cutlasses.

Ricketts and Morbeau were rubbing them with sand and rag, while the other two carefully "honed" those that were cleaned with long stones.

"By the piper!" said Ricketts, "we shall give 'em a surprise in the morning, and then, my hearties, the gold is ours. If I ever hungered for a job it's to settle that Jim Bentley. Such a dandy seaman— so soft-spoken, so nice—and a pet o' the captain's. I don't forget what I owe him for this."

He rolled up his shirt-sleeve, showing his left arm bandaged just below the elbow in the fleshy part.

"How's it getting on?" asked Morbeau.

"Oh! it'll heal, only the flesh is touchy," growled Ricketts. "But it was a close shave—the bullet went clean through it."

Turning to the other two men, he asked—

"Will you get an edge on 'em, you Dribble and Smitch?"

"Like a razor," answered a beetle-browed ruffian who had a right to the latter name.

"Mine's a bit notchy," said Dribble, with a grin, "but it will serve for the thick skull of the captain."

This was considered a good joke, for they all laughed aloud.

From within the cavern came back a most

sonorous echo—a booming and a rolling strange to hear.

"Darn that place!" growled Ricketts, looking back behind him. "I never heard anything like it."

"So big a trumpet to speak," said Morbeau.

"It's my belief there's some infernal jabbering spirit there," returned Ricketts. "Listen—hear me speak low. Hello, there!"

He stooped forward so as to get his head near the mouth of the cave, and in a whisper uttered the last two words.

The echo did not return immediately—possibly half a minute elapsed before it came back, with a slight swishing sound, "Hello, there!"

"That's a nice place to sleep in," observed Ricketts.

"It is ze only vun zat slope rising," said Morbeau; "all oders go down—tide roll in—ugh!"

"Anyway," replied Ricketts, "it's only for one night more. We'll take up our quarters aboard the Lapwing, and sleep on gold two nights hence."

"And take their stores, too," added Dribble, with a hungry look. "It's years since I felt the pangs of hunger so sharp. Here, let's have a biscuit."

He went into the cave, and soon appeared with a ship's biscuit in his hand.

It was one of the small store Captain Broadman had bestowed upon Dan Ricketts.

"Go easy with the grub," grumbled Ricketts; "we mayn't be able, after all, to get aboard the Lapwing for a day or two."

"Eat to-day and starve to-morrow," replied Dribble.

It was late in the afternoon just then, and, the sun was setting in the sea away to their right.

It was a glorious tropical sunset, and one that would have moved most people to admiration, but these men only looked at it with a sailor's eye.

"Rough weather coming," said Smitch. "I reckon there's a squall mixed up in that peculiar sky."

"Not yet, for a day or so," replied Ricketts; "it's only opening the ball."

There were four cutlasses now ready, and the edges having been tried and pronounced satisfactory, the rest were put away in the cave.

Each man took one of the sharpened swords and carried it with him.

A short distance inside the cave was a quantity of broken wood, from which the men proceeded to make a fire.

"It's plaguey smoky," said Smitch, "and confoundedly dirty, but it's risky having it outside."

When the fire was lighted they lay around it at their ease.

Not having any pipes, they were obliged to content themselves with chewing tobacco, of which each had a small supply—not in the best condition, thanks to the salt water that had got into their tin boxes.

"It's slow work lying here," said Smitch. "Who'll spin a yarn."

"Not me, with a devil yonder to jabber it back again," replied Dan Ricketts.

He cast a shuddering look into the depths of the cave, black as the blackest night.

Of the extent of it none of them knew aught, but they could tell by its appearance that it went far into the high ground overhead.

" Why not take a bundle of sticks and see what we can make of it ?"

" You can go," growled Ricketts, stretching himself out upon his back, "and if you get lost, as fellows have done in the great cave of Kentucky, that's your look-out."

Smitch and Dribble laughed as they got upon their feet, and for awhile busied themselves in selecting from a heap of loose wood a number of sticks with knots that resembled pine.

They were very resinous, and burnt freely.

" We'll burn half going," said Smitch, " and then, if we don't find the end, we'll burn the other half coming back again."

Ricketts and Morbeau lay side by side for awhile, occasionally exchanging a word, but, as it all came back to them in that dreadful echoing way, Ricketts at length got upon his feet, saying—

" Let's go outside and talk—I've something to say to you."

Morbeau got up, and then sauntered from the cave into the starlight.

The tide was out, and they could just see the outline of the old wreck, that had lain there probably for nearly a hundred years.

" It's getting mighty rotten," said Ricketts, " and will soon go to pieces now. It isn't safe to walk about it with heavy boots."

" Is zat vat you come here for to say ?" asked Morbeau, drily.

" No. Perhaps you guess what it is ?"

" Smitch and Dribble."

" Yes."

They both stood silent for a few moments, and

"Two fools !" he said ; "they couldn't be trusted."

"No," answered Morbeau, deliberately, "not *alive.*"

"Ah! you've hit it," said Ricketts, clutching him by the arm. "When the captain and that Jim is settled two will be enough to share—eh ?"

"It is so."

"Then we understand each other, Morbeau. Who's your man ?"

"Smitch."

"And Dribble's mine. It's settled. Hands on it."

They shook hands, and the unholy compact was sealed.

When the first bit of cowardly assassination was carried out Smitch and Dribble were to be the next victims.

And after that ?

Well, Morbeau had made up his mind to murder Ricketts, and Ricketts was determined to kill Morbeau—that's all.

A simple sum of reduction until only one remained as master of the spoil.

CHAPTER IX.

THE ATTACK ON THE LAPWING—DYNAMITE PUT TO A GOOD USE—JIM IS SORELY PUZZLED.

EFORE sunrise on the following morning Captain Broadman and Jim were awake and stirring. It was necessary that they should be so to watch the rise of the tide.

Both had built great hopes on the Lapwing being once more got afloat, and, wreck as it was, made to respond to the wind and answer to the helm. No matter how slowly they traversed the ocean, they would every day be nearer to the track of vessels—their only chance of final rescue.

In addition, the captain had other thoughts in his mind to which he did not give expression. Jim only thought of getting away from the island. Cooped-up as he was, he had already learned to hate it.

So these two were watching the in-coming tide when the captain, happening to raise his eyes to the summit of the cliff, saw the form of a man lying on the verge of it.

He got his glass and directed it towards the object, and to his startled vision appeared the form of Dan Ricketts, insensible or stone dead.

"Jim, my lad," he said, "summat's wrong up there. I hit that Ricketts after all, and he's crawled back to the cliff to die."

Then he looked at Jim, and Jim looked at him.

"It would be a shame to let a dog die and give him no help."

"It would, Captain Broadman."

"My lad," said the worthy old seaman, "it's my work that laid him low, and it's for me to put it right. I'll go up to him."

"Captain Broadman, suppose there should be some treachery?" urged Jim.

"It's only man to man if it comes to that," was the reply.

The captain, as he spoke, lowered the ladder, and descending it with a hasty step went straight for the cliff. Choosing the same track Jim had used when he took up the bag of biscuits, he soon began the ascent.

Then a most astounding and startling thing occurred, for which Jim was totally unprepared.

Four men came round from the *ocean* side of the Lapwing and made a dash at the rope-ladder.

In the foremost he recognised his old enemy, Dan Ricketts.

A very strong head might have been bewildered by the appearance of one who was apparently lying dead on the cliff above, but immediately the truth flashed upon Jim.

That figure was a dummy constructed to decoy one of the occupants of the Lapwing away and leave the other at the mercy of the assailants.

Add to this the bewildering effect of the appearance of three others, whom Jim believed to be dead and under the sea, and you may appreciate his emotion at that moment.

Dan Ricketts was half way up the ladder when Jim recovered himself, and, drawing his cutlass, he

Jim was a novice in the art of war, but Captain Broadman had taught him many tricks with the cutlass. Dan Ricketts was not at all prepared for Jim's display of determination, and, halting near the top of the ladder, he observed—

"You had better give in and be friends. If you only act reasonable you won't be hurt."

"Come one step further," said Jim, "and I will cut you down."

"Forward! *mon ami*," yelled Morbeau, from below.

He, like other Frenchmen, preferred a dash. Steady work discomposed him.

Thus urged, Dan Ricketts ascended another round of the ladder, but Jim, leaning over the side, so cut and slashed at him that he had to crouch down, and altogether cut a very sorry figure.

"I tell you we don't want to hurt you," said Ricketts.

"I'll not trust you," replied Jim. "You are rascals all, and I know not how many are behind you."

Then he bethought himself of a dynamite cartridge which lay handy, and picking it up he tossed off the rags and held it aloft.

"See this?" he said.

"Yes—a tin of sardines!" roared Dan Ricketts, and the others laughed.

"It is a dynamite cartridge," cried Jim, "and I give you while I count five to clear out. One!"

They all laughed again—it seemed to be so good a joke to try an idle scare on them.

"Vere shall you get ze dynamite?" asked the Frenchman. "Ah! yes; you make him in ze frying-

JIM DASHED DOWN UPON THE RUFFIAN.

"Two !" cried Jim.

"Oh! don't take the trouble to count," said Ricketts, from his position half-way up the ladder; "save your breath for another game."

"Three !" said Jim.

He fixed his eye upon a stone a few yards from the ship, at which he would aim the cartridge.

He knew the action of dynamite. It would explode downward, and probably not injure the ship, but it would at least give Dribble and Smitch, who stood near it, a hoist into the air and a scare.

Somehow the resolute air of Jim began to tell upon Dan Ricketts, who, after casting an apprehensive glance around, displayed an inclination to descend to *terra firma*.

But Morbeau only yelled at him, and bade him let a *man* come into his place. Thus taunted, Dan Ricketts returned to the charge.

"Four !—FIVE !" cried Jim, and then, with a faultless aim, he cast the cartridge down upon the stone.

The explosion that followed was not so very great, but it tried the nerves nevertheless.

A cloud of sand and stones was hurled into the air, and mingled with it were the fragments of Dribble's body.

The full force of the explosion had caught him and rent him asunder as if he had been a figure of paper and lath.

Smitch was blown backwards and turned clean over, but was unhurt, Morbeau was cast to the right and violently dashed against the side of the ship, while Dan Ricketts fell from the ladder as if he had been shot.

dynamite, for he was thrown across the deck of the vessel and landed against the side of it.

For a few moments he was stunned, and had Ricketts known of his condition the capture of the Lapwing would have been an easy affair.

But the scoundrel and his two companions had vanished from the scene so completely that when, a minute later, the captain came tumbling down the cliff, and Jim staggered back to his old position of defence, all that remained was the scattered fragments of Dribble's body.

To the captain it seemed as if Ricketts had been blown to pieces, for there were the ghastly pieces of evidence around of somebody having suffered; but when Jim had explained everything it was the old seaman's opinion that he was not the victim of the explosion.

"Morbeau, Dribble, Smitch, and Ricketts," he mused; " an ugly combination—but one is gone. And where are the other three ?"

It was a puzzle, for by ordinary means of locomotion they could not have got out of sight. That they were hiding somewhere seemed the most reasonable solution of the puzzle.

"Fetch the rifles, lad," said Captain Broadman. "I'll watch until you come back. Be sharp, and maybe we may be able to get a pot shot at 'em. After what's happened this morning I'll show as much mercy as I would to skunks, no more."

Jim got the rifles, and with these cocked and ready they kept on the look-out for the vanished men for fully half an hour.

No sign of them rewarded their efforts, nor for the next two hours when they took it in turns to

"They lie close," said Captain Broadman, "or they've got away by some means unbeknown to us."

Meanwhile the tide had come in and risen much higher than it had done before. It washed right up to the base of the cliff, and the Lapwing half lifted itself in the buoyant water.

But there was not enough of it to float her, and she slowly settled down again.

"To-morrow she'll lift easier than I expected," said Captain Broadman, exultingly. "We must try and get a bit of canvas of some sort set to-day. To work, my lad."

Jim felt his spirits rise at the prospect, and, hurrying down to the store-room, he brought up some spare sails and rope, and a topmast was got out of the hold.

Captain Broadman worked with him, but in such a manner that he could at any moment have a look round for the vanished men.

The morning passed, and yet there were no signs of them. Deeper and deeper became the mystery of their disappearance.

"Maybe they were blown up, and are lying dead somewhere," said Jim.

"Then let them lie," returned the old seaman, "if that's what's come to 'em; but I've my doubts. Hark! my lad—the voices."

It was the first time they had heard them during the day, but there they were, distinct enough to the ear, though strangely muffled still.

By the tones it was comparatively easy to judge that the speakers were cursing each other for the ill-fortune that had attended their attack upon the Lapwing.

"Where are they?" asked Jim, bewildered.

"Pretty nigh," replied the captain, vaguely.

A few moments later the voices softened down, and finally stopped, but after the lapse of half an hour they were heard again.

Ceasing work, the two men stood side by side, endeavouring to find the exact spot from which the sounds came.

Suddenly the face of the captain brightened up, and he pointed towards the face of the cliff, about ten feet from the ground.

"They are there," he said.

"Where?" exclaimed Jim, amazed.

He could see nothing but broken rocks, with a few coarse weeds growing in the interstices. Apparently nothing bigger than a rabbit could have hidden away in such a spot.

"Take the cue from me," said the captain, "and talk loud. I want 'em to hear. The badger's got to be drawn."

"I don't see where from," observed Jim with a smile.

With their rifles in their hands they went down the ladder, and Captain Broadman led the way up the cliff, talking louder than was absolutely necessary.

"You may depend on it, lad," he said, "that they are all killed, and the island's our own. We can do a bit of roaming, and I think we'd better haul the place over. The ship won't come to no harm while we're away."

"No, I suppose not," said Jim, taking up the cue.

But still he could not see what sort of kite the captain was flying.

"Dead and gone, the lot of 'em!" chuckled the old seaman. "Ha! ha! and never a bit o' the lucre in the old hulk will they touch—"

He stopped suddenly, touched Jim on the arm, and pointed to a level part of a cliff, like a very small table-land, just above a biggish stone.

"There—SIT," he said, in the lightest of whispers.

Jim obeyed him because he had promised to do so, but for the life of him he could not see what his object was.

A fear that trouble and excitement had unhinged the mind of the old seaman took possession of him.

And this feeling was intensified when Broadman pursued his way singing the fragment of an old sea song.

"What on earth does he mean by it?" muttered Jim.

But, mindful of instructions, he kept quite still, and presently the captain ceased singing.

Then Jim saw him cautiously returning.

With scarce a sound he reached his side, and, putting his lips close to Jim's ear, he whispered—

"Stay there, and don't move half an inch for your life, if you have to wait all day and all night. *We've got 'em!*"

CHAPTER X.

THE ROBBERS' CAVE—JIM TOO IMPETUOUS—THE EVER-RISING TIDE.

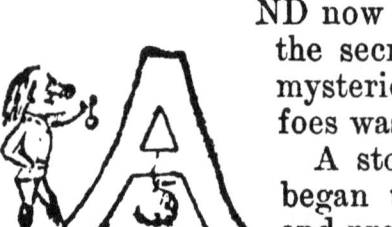

ND now it flashed upon Jim that the secret of the voices and the mysterious disappearance of his foes was about to be revealed.

A stone of considerable size began to shift slowly forward, and presently two coarse, knotty hands were seen to be projecting.

Then came a pause.

"What you see—anything?" asked a voice, which Jim recognised as that of Morbeau the cook.

"They've left the ship," answered the hoarse voice of Dan Ricketts, "jest as I told you. Gone aloft to look about for us."

"Now is our time. Eh—is it so?"

"Right, monseer. But we must go cautiously. There's no knowing what tricks they are up to. I wonder where they got that blamed dynamite from?"

"Go on board and see."

"Steady it is."

The stone was pushed further out and then suddenly set off rolling downwards, falling upon the soft sand below with a dull thud.

"Now, then—out," cried Morbeau.

"Confound it! lie still a moment," answered Ricketts; "they may have heard or seen it go. Give 'em time to look round a bit."

Jim and Captain Broadman never stirred, save that Jim extended his arms ready to pounce upon Ricketts as soon as he fairly showed himself.

But he was in no hurry to do so.

With the superlative cunning of a knave, he thought it possible that Jim and the captain, who he believed had gone up to the summit of the cliff, might be endeavouring to make out what had shifted the stone, and, if they saw nothing, would attribute it to an ordinary little landslip common to cliff-bound shores.

Not hearing any sound, he at length concluded he might creep out, and slowly half his body emerged from its hiding-place.

"Pin him!" cried the captain.

hands seizing him by the neck ; but in his eagerness he forgot that he was above his intended prey, and the consequence was he turned fairly head over heels, jamming the face of Dan Ricketts against the ground with considerable violence.

But he had to let go, and Ricketts, though bleeding and blinded with dust, darted backwards into his hiding-place like a worm touched with a stick.

He narrowly escaped a blow aimed at him by the captain with the butt-end of his rifle.

Down dashed the old salt, and as soon as he could get into position he fired into the hole, when a roar such as might have come from a giant speaking-trumpet followed.

Whether anybody was hurt it was impossible to say, for in the case of a wounded man crying out his voice would have been lost amid the echoes raised in the cave.

Jim was now up again, very much exasperated with himself for being so impetuous, but the captain laughed good-naturedly, saying—

" You did your best, my lad—in fact you over-did it."

" How did those blackguards discover such a place as this ?" asked Jim.

" Aye, that wants thinking out," replied the old seaman ; " but I guess I have the bearings of it. Put your ear down by the hole—you needn't be afraid to do so.   They've got no firearms and have cleared off by this time."

Jim was not afraid.   Kneeling he listened.

" What do you hear ?"

" A thumping of feet walking quickly."

"Coming or going ?"

" Going."

"What else?"

"The swishing of the sea upon the shore, or something like it."

"Just so, my lad. There lies the whole thing in a nutshell. This is a part of the island where the sea has encroached on the other side of it, and gradually scooped out a vein of soft soil until it has *nearly* got through to here. I don't say it was done to day—or yesterday—or a hundred years ago. In the making of things Nature doesn't count time."

"I begin to see now," observed Jim. "And these fellows found the cave and discovered how near it brought them to us."

"Just so," returned the captain. "Now, if you look at this hole, you will notice that the stone didn't quite fit. Why not? Because the rain from above, running down, has washed some of the soil away, letting daylight in; but the cracks weren't big enough for us to notice from the Lapwing."

"And yet wide enough to let the voices out," said Jim.

"Of course, and what's more, that 'ere cave is about one of the biggest and best speaking-trumpets on earth. Ever been in China?"

"No—I've been nowhere except with you," was the answer.

"Oh! well—there they make this kind of thing artificial, so that when the wind is blowing they make such howling rows as you have never dreamt of. I'll tell you more about 'em by and bye. For the present we will get back to the ship."

On descending they noticed that the tide was fully up—higher than ever. To get to the Lapwing they had to wade up to their knees at the start, and by the time they got to the ladder the water was round their waists.

"Never mind, Jim," said the captain; "if this goes on we may float to-morrow. Look at the old craft. See how uneasy she is."

There was indeed a creaking and groaning going on all over her, as if she were trying to "lift herself" from the ground.

As Jim was climbing up the ladder he fancied the vessel also slightly rocked.

They hauled the ladder up, and busied themselves in getting up their rigging ready for the hoped-for start on the morrow.

As for Ricketts and those with him, they would be well content to leave them on the island—a more miserable fate their bitterest enemy could not have wished them.

Nor was there any fear of their attempting to attack the vessel again—at least, none that the captain could see—and he smoked the pipe of contentment that day.

"To-morrow, my lad—to-morrow," he said. "The wind's been steady across the island, and if it doesn't shift we shall float."

"Isn't there anything we can lighten her of?" suggested Jim.

"Not much that would help us. But it's a good thought. There's the seamen's chests and such like; we can pitch 'em over the side. If those chaps stay on here they will want a change of clothes."

It was a small joke, but they both laughed at it, for their hearts were light.

You see, they had such high hopes of the next day.

CHAPTER XI.

THE ANGRY CONSPIRATORS—A NEW PLOT—A WALK THROUGH THE MIST—A CRUEL DEED—DISAPPOINTED PLOTTERS.

FEW sights are more unpleasant than a thoroughly angry man raging and fuming, but when he has the qualities and appearance of a blackguard and scoundrel the effect is hideous.

Morbeau, Smitch, and Ricketts had escaped unhurt from the captain's rifle, but they were in a state of madness over the failure of their expedition.

The full extent of the cave, as the reader may guess, had been discovered by Smitch and Dribble on that night when they went exploring with their bundle of torches.

A further inspection by the whole party the next day showed them little streams of daylight coming through, and a glimpse of the Lapwing had been obtained.

Such a rare piece of luck had seldom fallen to the lot of adventurers.

Then Dan Ricketts conceived the plan of making a dummy of himself to draw the captain up the cliff, and it was done with the clothing of the one solitary

It was such a notable scheme from their point of view that they felt certain of success.

But it failed, as other notable schemes have done from time immemorial.

After the explosion of the dynamite-cartridge the three survivors managed to get back to their hiding-place before Jim recovered from the shock. The stone which they had loosened to let themselves out was pulled back into its place, and through one of the chinks Ricketts watched the bewilderment of Jim and the captain.

"We aren't licked yet," he said. "Bide a bit and we'll get aboard the Lapwing sure."

So they lay close, watching until the time came when Jim and the captain were seen to start up the cliff—as the three surviving rascals hoped—in search of themselves.

How far they were right and what followed we know.

The rage of these men over their double failure was ludicrous.

They raged, stamped, swore, and reviled each other and everything for a long time, but at length a calmer state of things prevailed.

"What's the good of it?" asked Ricketts. "Let's talk business. Smitch, sit down, and you, Morbeau, leave off dancing like a cat on hot bricks."

"Vot good business you talk?" demanded Morbeau. "Shall ve not lose 'em—eh? Why is it they put up mast? Tell me."

"Of course I know their game," replied Ricketts, "to get afloat with the high tides. But look here, we 'ave got some old axes out of the other wreck, haven't we?"

"Yes."

" And several of 'em is pointed like pickaxes, I believe."

" Aint we seen 'em ?" sulkily demanded Smitch.

" Of course you have, thickhead," replied Ricketts. " Well, what's the good of 'em, you say? Why this—to punch half a dozen holes in the bottom of the Lapwing—that will stop her floating long if she rises at all. Now, then ?"

" And while we are doing that what will *they* be up to ?" asked Smitch.

" Let 'em be up to what they like," replied Ricketts ; " I'm game to try my luck at it to-night. Can't we creep close, and all together give one—two blows with them axes—and won't that be enough ?—and then skedaddle ?"

" What time ?"

" Let me see. High tide to-night is about ten o'clock ; well, at eleven we will be on the road. They won't look for us with water about. But we must go round the point of the island and not by that derned cave ; that'll do 'em another way. Now what do you think of it ?"

" It can be done," said Morbeau.

" And if we can keep 'em here," continued Ricketts, " don't you think we three can get hold o' them two afore long? Wake up, Smitch, and get some o' them axes out from that hulk."

Smitch woke up in a fashion and shuffled off to the old wreck. He climbed up the sloping deck and disappeared down the aft companion.

" He is only one man," remarked Ricketts. When we get our ship we must share him between us."

" A blow in front, a blow behind, and it is over," said Morbeau.

In a few minutes Smitch returned, bringing with him half a dozen axes with spikes on the heads— old-fashioned boarding weapons, used for cutting away obstructions and stabbing a foe.

They set to work cleaning them—more to kill time than of necessity, for the points, though rusty, could easily be thrust through an ordinary piece of timber.

In this work they passed the day.

When night was at hand they began their journey to the point. They had not far to go, but the way was rough, and there was a mist over the sea near the setting sun that they thought would settle on the island.

"It will be welcome by and bye," said Ricketts, "for it will cover us when at work."

This was a comforting thought. Nature for once seemed to play into their hands, and their hearts grew lighter than they had been since they were thrown upon the island.

Morbeau even went so far as to cut a caper. It takes very little to set a Frenchman dancing.

The elements of joy lie mostly in their lower extremities. An Englishman is merry with his head.

They reached the point of the island, where the mist was beginning to gather around them. Darkness would soon be there, and then they could go on.

"The tide is rolling in," said Smitch. "We ought to be near the vessel now."

"Pshaw!" said the sanguine Ricketts, "what matters? Is not the cliff all broken up here? We shall not drown."

Deeper grew the mist, and with it came darkness —as there were no stars it was the darkness of the tomb.

Still there was no cause for anxiety.

They could grope their way along, guided by the murmuring of the sea.

They started for the Lapwing at last, each man carrying his axe, and when they spoke scarcely raising their voices above a whisper.

"We shall not be expected to-night," said Ricketts.

"*Parbleu!*" replied Morbeau—"no."

The way was getting rough.

To avoid the incoming waters they kept among the broken ground, feeling their way over great boulders, and occasionally falling, but not to hurt themselves to any degree.

At length Smitch slipped, and fell so as to get himself wedged between two pieces of rock. He cried out that he was fixed for life, and the others, cursing, bade him hold his tongue.

"We will have you out, my friend," said Morbeau, "only be still."

They felt their way to him, and, having got at his arms and legs, tugged away without lifting him an inch.

"It cannot be done till the daylight comes," said Ricketts.

"It comes to this, then," added Morbeau—"he must rest here until we return."

But Smitch cried out that he would not be left, and his voice sounded dismal and hollow in the fog. Once more they bade him be quiet.

"You won't hurt," said Ricketts. "The tide will never reach you."

"I don't know that," he answered. "If you don't get me out I'll yell my loudest, and then, perhaps, they will hear me on board the Lapwing."

"Stay," answered Morbeau, "we will try to find a way to free you."

He drew aside with Ricketts, and the pair held a whispered consultation together.

"What is to be done, Morbeau?"

"Ah! what? See, now he is fixed—helpless—and of little use—"

"But then we shall only be two left."

"What of that—two against two—and we may get at them divided. Be a man. It is better to kill one and not see him than to look upon his wounds."

"You do it, Morbeau."

"Nay, we will share in it. Let us draw lots. I will pick up a stone. I have it. Now it is in one of my hands. Touch. If you get the hand with the stone you must do it. If that hand is left for me, the task is mine."

He thrust his two closed hands against the breast of Ricketts as he spoke, and one was seized and held.

"Open," said Ricketts.

The Frenchman did so slowly, and there was a stone in the palm.

"It is for you to do it," exclaimed Morbeau.

Ricketts shivered.

He did not care for the task under the circumstances. It seemed something particularly diabolical to grope about for a man, to feel your way to the very spot, and then to strike and kill him.

But he had accepted the idea of drawing lots, and it must be done.

Morbeau stood by grinning in the misty gloom.

He had picked up TWO stones, and with one in either hand had juggled the dreadful business.

And Dan Ricketts, who thought he was cleverer than most men, had not the wit to suspect.

"Come," said Morbeau, "hasten. Don't shirk it."

"It is so horrible," muttered Ricketts. "If we leave him—"

"Leave him to yell and raise alarm, so we get more dynamite. Pah!"

"I'll do it!" groaned Ricketts.

"Smitch," he said, aloud, "where are you? Speak a little, so that I—we—may find you."

"I'm here," moaned Smitch. "It seems to me that these stones are shifting and pressing against me. I'm choking."

Then Ricketts felt his way to him, and, guided by his moans, laid a hand upon his head.

"Ah! here you are," he said.

"Quick!" hissed Morbeau.

And then it was done.

A single blow from that dreadful axe sufficed, and one of the cruellest and most cowardly of deeds ever conceived by man was perpetrated.

Ricketts sank upon his knees, and for a moment covered his face with his hands. He felt from that moment he was a man accursed.

Morbeau presently spoke again.

"Vhat you do?" he said. "Vill it not be time to-morrow to rob his pockets?"

"I am not robbing him," hurriedly replied Ricketts. "I could not touch him—I dare not look upon his face again."

He got up and stumbled towards his companion, who, as they touched each other, seized him by the arm.

"After all," said Morbeau, "you are a chicken, my friend."

"I am as good a man as you are," replied Ricketts. "Let us get away from here."

They crept on, listening to the lapping of the sea as it ran up the shore, and it was the only sound they heard for awhile.

Then a soft moaning fell upon their ears.

"Smitch!" exclaimed Ricketts, with a gasp—"he is not dead!"

"You fool!" growled Morbeau, "it is ze vind. It is coming, and by and bye ze mist go. Ah! zen for vork alone."

"Let us go on," groaned Ricketts.

It was some time ere they spoke again—not until they thought they must be near the Lapwing; then Ricketts proposed they should leave the rougher ground and go down to the smoother beach.

Morbeau assented, and they descended to the sands. The water had just reached the spot and rushed round their feet.

On they went, cautiously and slowly, their eyes straining ahead to get a glimpse of the huge hulk, for dark as it might be surely they would be able to see a faint outline of it.

Morbeau suggested they should take to the rougher ground again, as the splashing of the water as they walked was likely to betray their coming.

"And we can't be far from it now," he said.

Ricketts was getting heartsick and weary—he wanted a rest.

"Let us sit down a bit," he said; "there is plenty of time."

There was, Morbeau admitted, and having got clear of the sea they sat down and rested.

The moaning overhead was increasing, the wind was rising, but the mist did not clear away so fast as they expected.

"There is no break in it," said Morbeau. "We

are in a fog that covers hundreds of miles, perhaps. It may be here until the sun rises.

Both were a little knocked up, being weak from want of food, and overcome by fatigue. They rested for an hour or more and then went on again.

"Surely we must be near her now,' said Ricketts, after a long spell of crawling.

"It may be so. I tink not," answered Morbeau. "But let us go down again."

Once more they went down to the water, and waded through it knee-deep.

A very high tide—it would be the highest they had known ere it had done flowing.

On, on, on, for a long time, and still no Lapwing.

Then there flashed a thought of what they had done upon Ricketts, and, pulling up, he said—

"We have come too far."

"I believe so," returned Morbeau.

"It is getting sickening," growled Ricketts. "This fog is dead against us."

"Let us wait until it rises," said Morbeau; "to me it is not so much as it was."

The fog did appear to be a little thinner—anyway, the wind was rising. They could hear it whistling among the trees on the summit of the cliff.

In bitterness of heart they again sought higher ground and rested, both lying down sullenly silent.

Presently it was quite clear that the fog was being dispersed, but just when it promised to disappear it thickened again.

Another fog-bank was being driven over the island.

So they kept where they were for another hour, only the time seemed longer, and they were beginning to think the day would soon be there when the fog rapidly cleared, showing them a sky full of stars.

Both were seamen enough to know the hour by the position of the Coal Sack and Southern Cross, and together they said—

"It is not yet midnight."

A glance around them failed to reveal the presence of the Lapwing, and then came the question whether they had come too far or had not travelled far enough.

"I say too far," said Morbeau.

So they retraced their steps, and, by the better light, walked fast in comparison to what they had done. The beach was still covered with water, but the tide was receding.

"Stop a minute," said Ricketts, pulling up. "After all, we did not go far enough. I think yonder is the spot where Smitch is lying."

"How you tell zat?" asked Morbeau. "You not see it dere?"

"I *feel* it," rejoined Ricketts, "and that is enough for me."

So back they went again, and now the water allowed them to travel on the more level ground.

With staring eyes fixed ahead they looked for the Lapwing, but failed to find her.

Presently Morbeau began to curse his companion for his folly and ask him why he had yielded to fancy.

"You only *tink* of Smitch; he vas not dere."

"We must put off the job until to-morrow," groaned Ricketts; "I am done up."

Morbeau was played out too, and together they began to climb the cliff to find some spot where they could lie close until there was daylight enough for them to see their way. They found a hollow in which to lie down. There was warmth in their hiding-place, and it being aided by fatigue they fell asleep

It is said that murderers cannot sleep, but Ricketts slept soundly, without dreams, until he found himself awakened by a rude shaking.

It was Morbeau who had aroused him, and, starting to his feet, he saw that it was broad day.

"*Sacre!* What fools we haf been!" hissed Morbeau.

"Not so loud," said Ricketts; "they may hear you on the Lapwing."

"Ah! yes," exclaimed Morbeau, in mocking tones, "vat ears dey must have. Look dere?"

He pointed out to sea. Ricketts, following his outstretched finger, beheld the hull of the vessel with a small square sail near the bow.

Thanks to a favourable tide and wind she was a good three or four miles away.

"Lifted with the tide!" roared Ricketts.

"It is so," said Morbeau, "and for you and me dere is—vhat—?"

"Starvation!" groaned Ricketts, as he fell flat upon his face on the floor of the hollow.

The cruel murder of Smitch was already half avenged.

CHAPTER XII.

THE LAPWING AFLOAT—SHORT OF WATER—A SAIL ON THE HORIZON—THE CAPTAIN DOGGED.

 ES, the Lapwing had floated off by the night-tide. Captain Broadman—whose watch it was—felt her lift, and as by that time he had the short mast and sail ready, he hoisted the latter and waited for the ship to move.

By slow degrees he felt the Lapwing rise and rise, then she began to grind her keel upon the sand, and finally floated off, free once more.

The old captain could see nothing, but he could hear the moaning of the wind above, and knew that once the vessel got away from the cliff that she would move along, slowly but surely, seaward.

Then, when the turn of the tide came, he would have something more in his favour, and overpowered by his emotion he knelt and breathed his thanks in the spirit of a devout man.

He did not doubt the seaworthiness of the Lapwing's hull, because he had pretty well overhauled her as late as the evening before. She was sound enough—being a very strong vessel of the good old sort—built of oak, and plenty of it.

The rudder was not hopelessly damaged either. It would answer for ordinary steering purposes, and he took up his position at the stern to keep her head in the proper direction.

"There'll been change in the watch to-night, my lad," he said, smilingly addressing the sleeping Jim.

Nor was there.

Without any sense of fatigue the captain kept his post long after the mist had cleared away and the stars shone out. He was there when Jim, just before sunrise, awoke with a start.

"Captain Broadman," he said, "it isn't fair."

"No, it isn't," replied the now jovial old man. "I ought not to have kept all the enjoyment to myself. I have been having a jolly night of it."

Jim stared about him for a moment bewildered. The vessel was heaving on the sea, blue water was on every side, while in the distance was the island.

"Got afloat a tide afore we reckoned on," said the captain. "Ah! my lad, we've a heap to be thankful for."

Jim turned away and leaning his elbows on the side of the vessel buried his face in his hands.

He remained thus for a few moments and then faced about again.

"I can take the helm now," he said; "you must want some rest."

"Get breakfast," replied the captain. "I'll sleep when I see that island no more than a cloud behind us. We shall make more headway directly—the wind is freshening."

Jim joyously went to work. Having lighted a fire in the galley he made some coffee, and while he was doing so he remembered one thing that might be of serious import by and bye.

They had but one cask of water on board.

It was a remnant of the old stock of the Lapwing.

On the island they had not been able to procure any, and in the excitement arising from the hope of getting away it had been forgotten.

But he decided not to mar the joy of the captain by naming it, and the breakfast being ready they both made a hearty meal, the helm being meanwhile lashed to keep the Lapwing headed north.

"I don't conceal from you, Jim," said the captain, "that we've got a slow voyage before us, but we'll get through it."

"How long shall we be?" asked Jim.

"All depends."

"If we fall in with a vessel there's an end of it, isn't there?"

"No—I want no vessels. My lad, I undertook to get the Lapwing to a certain spot with certain stores aboard her, and I'm going to do it. This wind won't shift for a month."

"A month!" exclaimed Jim. "Shall we be as long as that?"

"Surely," replied the captain, composedly; "two, it may be. But we have stores aboard for four."

"Yes," said Jim.

Two months, and only one cask of water!

How strange of the captain, with his experience, to overlook a thing so serious!

That he had overlooked it was certain, and Jim resolved not to breathe a word about it while the subject could be avoided.

After breakfast the captain got out his telescope and had a look at the island behind him. It was a good glass, as we have said before, and it enabled him to make out Morbeau and Ricketts just after the latter had learnt about the departure of the Lapwing.

"A heavy judgment has fallen on those fellows. Honest men could have come away with us, but they have to remain behind—to starve, I fear. I don't like the meanest of men coming to *that* end."

"It must be horrible," said Jim.

"Nothing like it."

"Not even dying of thirst?"

"Oh! that's worse."

After this Jim was silent for a time, and then he began to sing.

It was past noon ere the island became cloudy enough for the captain to lie down to sleep, and when he did he slept but two hours.

Jim meanwhile had taken the helm, and steered north-by-west, as the captain had directed him.

It was a glorious afternoon—sunny, and with a fresh breeze. Jim's keen eyes, a few moments before the captain woke up, had seen a speck rising above the horizon, due north. As in duty bound, he called the attention of the captain to it.

Once more the glass was brought into requisition, and after a steady look at the object the captain walked forward and began to lower the sail.

"Let go of her helm," he said to Jim; "let her float as she likes."

"What is it?" asked Jim. "A pirate?"

"No—a trader, and a big one. She'll go on if we look like a derelict. Those fellows haven't mite to go out of their course to inspect a ship that looks like a log."

"But would it not be better if she saw us?" asked Jim.

"You do as you are told," said the captain, with a dogged face. "Who's captain on board the Lap-

"Why you are, sir."

"And you are under me, aint you?"

"Yes, sir."

"Then obey orders, and don't you ask any fool's questions, please. I know what I'm doing."

He spoke somewhat roughly, after the manner of captains when their authority is questioned, but he softened again in a moment.

"Do as you are told, my lad," he said; "it will be all right in the end."

"Shall I tell him of the one cask of water now thought Jim.

And then a feeling came over him that if the captain could be obstinate why so could he.

So he was dumb.

Meanwhile the whole of the sails and the hull of the big vessel had risen above the horizon.

CHAPTER XIII.

THE CAPTAIN WON'T BE RESCUED—JIM MORE AND MORE PUZZLED.

IM could not understand the old captain at all. The majority of people would have rejoiced to find there was a chance of being rescued from such a perilous position, but he plainly exhibited a terror of any help being afforded him.

The vessel drew near, and by a slight alteration in her course showed that she had seen the Lapwing and intended to bear down upon her. There could, in a sailor's mind, be no doubt about it.

"Stick to the helm, Jim," cried the captain,

"and do just as I tell you.   Hard a-port!   We've got to bear away from her."

Jim ported the helm with a stifled groan.   It seemed to him like committing suicide, and he was far from feeling a desire to die just yet.

But, port the helm as he might, the Lapwing could not get away from the stranger—nor, indeed, from an ordinary boat—as the wind had lulled, and she was barely moving through the water.

Presently the stranger was near enough for Jim to see the seamen in the bows and the officers in the stern scanning the Lapwing, and, having got right across the track of the wreck, the well-canvassed craft was brought-to and a boat lowered.

Captain Broadman rushed below, and Jim had barely time to wonder what move he was up to now when he reappeared with his speaking-trumpet in his hand.

"Keep off!" he roared ; "we don't want you."

"But, Captain Broadman," said Jim, "don't you think we shall be better if we are taken off?"

"No, I don't," replied the captain, angrily. "Look here, my lad, you trust to me. I'm not so mad as you may think. Anyway, if I am, 'there's method in my madness,' as I once heard a play-acting chap say. Stand by the wheel and obey orders, or, by the lord, I'll chop you down as a mutineer."

"I suppose he knows what he's up to," groaned Jim. "Anyway, he can do as he likes."

As the boat, with half a dozen men in her, drew near, the old captain roared again and again for it to stand off.

"You aint wanted here!" he yelled through his trumpet.

JIM WAS STARTLED BY THE SIGHT OF A SWARTHY SAVAGE APPROACHING HIM.

But the boat still came on, and presently touched the sides of the Lapwing.

Captain Broadman dashed down the speaking-trumpet, and, drawing his cutlass, got ready to stop the boarding of his vessel.

"The first man who comes aboard I'll chine," he cried.

"Go easy, mate," cried a voice from below. "We'll take you off and look after you."

"I don't want you," cried the captain.

Two heads appeared above the side of the vessel, and the old seaman struck at them with a determination that caused both to promptly disappear.

Then the captain went to the side, and, leaning upon his arms, looked calmly down into the boat.

A man, dressed as the mate of a merchantman, and half a dozen ordinary seamen were there. One and all eyed him in a round-eyed, startled way.

"Look here, my friends," said the captain, quietly enough, "I've said I don't want you, and I don't mean to have you. Who are you to come boarding a man's ship against his will?"

"We thought you were in trouble, and came to help you," replied the mate.

"Thank you kindly for that much," said the captain, "but we are well provisioned, and I mean to get my craft into port without paying salvage on her."

"What port?"

"That's my affair."

"It strikes me," said the mate, "that you are an old fool. What does your young mate say?"

"Where's the rest of the crew?"

"Deserted us."

"Hi! there, young 'un—you at the wheel," cried the mate, "do you want to stop aboard this hulk?"

Jim did hesitate a little before replying, but it was scarcely perceptible.

"Yes—I stand by him," he answered.

"All right, then," said the mate. "If you are a pair of jackasses that's your look-out; we haven't any time to fool about after you. Give way there!"

The boat was pushed off, and the men, bending to their oars, rowed smartly back to the vessel.

They climbed on board, the boat was hoisted in, and once more she veered to the wind and resumed her voyage.

The tack she was on brought her quite close to the Lapwing, and as she passed her side was lined with officers and men staring at her.

Captain Broadman, leaning against the stump of the foremast, calmly lit a cigar and waved his hand to the captain of the other vessel, who was seated aft quietly smoking his weed.

No response was made to this salute, and the vessels were soon wide apart.

In an hour, spent by Broadman in watching the movements of the stranger, she was well down on the horizon.

"That's been a merciful escape," he said, wiping his forehead. "I hope we shall not have the ill-luck to fall in with any more of 'em."

"You will excuse me, Captain Broadman," inter-

"No doubt, no doubt," answered the captain, "but you will have it all cleared up by and bye."

"And there is one thing I ought to have mentioned before, perhaps," pursued Jim; "we have only one cask of water on board."

"Only one cask?" said the captain, thoughtfully; "thirty-six gallons. Well, we can do with half a gallon a day betwixt us, and that's enough for seventy-two days. I think it will be sufficient, my lad. Now I'll take the helm a bit, and you prepare something to eat, for after that bit of a rumpus with those fellows I feel as if I wanted it."

"Seventy-two days," thought Jim, as he yielded up the wheel. "He talks as if we were likely to be months at sea in this old tub. Perhaps I had better have gone with those fellows—and yet I wouldn't desert him. Right or wrong in his head, I'll stand by him."

But the look-out was rather queer, and Jim could not help giving vent to a sigh over the prospect before him.

"FOURTEEN days," thought Jim; "it seems more like fourteen months."

He was standing forward, the captain at the helm, looking out upon what was in his eyes simply an extension of an apparently interminable sea.

A fortnight had elapsed since they saw the vessel that offered them help, and since then they had looked upon nothing but sky and sea.

All the time a steady wind had been blowing from the same quarter as when the Lapwing started from the island, to the great delight of Captain Broadman.

"It's sent for us," he would say twenty times a day; "we are bound to be in port within a month."

But what port?

Jim asked himself this question again and again, but there was no answer. His companion kept the destination of the Lapwing a secret for reasons that will presently appear.

"Jim," he sang out, from the wheel.

"Aye, aye—sir," replied Jim, in the old style.

"I think, my lad, we are going to have a bit of a blow," said the captain.

Jim locked around. There was not a cloud in sight, not an extra ripple on the sea, no sign of any change.

"Do you think so?" he replied, dubiously.

"Jim," returned the captain, after a pause, "I feel it's coming. Run down and look at the barometer. You'll believe that if you won't believe me."

Jim smiled and hastened below. A glance at the barometer showed him that it was falling rapidly.

He came up with the intelligence stamped upon his face, and the old captain laughed with glee.

"You are like the rest of the world," he said. "You can understand a thing of wood and glass, filled with a bit of quicksilver that can't be seen, but you won't give flesh and blood credit for the same thing."

"I shall believe it in future," replied Jim.

"Now the blow that is coming," said the captain, "is coming from the right quarter, and if our canvas will only hold we shall put on a good extra sixty knots before morning. There'll be rain, too —not a shower, but buckets full. Look aft, my lad."

Jim looked aft, and saw a small cloud, shaped like a balloon, rising above the horizon.

"There's water in that, enough for a small deluge," said the captain, "but there will be wind after it. Now everything must be battened down close, or we may get the craft filled with water. I've seen these storms before. You had better go below."

"Why?" asked Jim.

"Well, it will save you getting wet."

"And you remain on deck?"

"Of course."

"Then I remain with you."

"Good lad," said the captain. "Now go to work. Batten everything down close, and what you don't want washed overboard chuck into the hold. You have half an hour before you. Take in our bit of canvas. It must be close hauled, and fasten it as if it's to hold for ever; then come here, and we'll splice ourselves to the wheel in case a wave or two should wash over us."

Jim saw that something more than he had hitherto been mixed up with was to be expected, and he looked forward to it with all the interest a man feels in that which may cost him his life.

With the hatches and companion closed and battened down he was ready for the fray.

Captain Broadman himself lashed the pair to the supports of the wheel.

By that time clouds, heavy and threatening, were well up in the sky, and presently the storm broke.

It gave no warning preliminary drops, but came upon them as a bucket of water might be thrown from a first-floor window.

The rain poured down at once like a cataract. The water rose up in a mist as it struck the deck, enveloping all ahead in a fog. The light of day was snuffed out and darkness came on—as if an extinguisher had been put over sun, moon, and stars.

With the rain came the wind—a hurricane.

The wisp of canvas which had been stretched forward was carried away as if it had been a puff of

The sea came up behind, and was breaking over the stern and sweeping the deck.

Well, indeed, it was for Jim that he had been lashed by a master hand, or he would have been carried over the vessel's side and away seaward to a watery grave.

But the cords held, and beyond a tremendous ducking and a temporary suspension of breath he experienced no inconvenience.

It amazed him to find how well the old hull of the ship stood the shock.

Instead of breaking up or sinking the Lapwing only trembled a bit, and then careered on before the storm.

Lightning now and thunder, heavier rain, and sea after sea over the deck!

An hour of this violence was followed by a better time. The rain fell lighter, but heavy enough still in all conscience, and, with longer gaps between, the lightning flashed and the thunder rolled. The sea alone maintained its aggressive power.

But even that in time showed a reduction of its force, although not until the storm was practically over and the clouds above cleared away.

The real night had come then and the sky was full of stars.

As soon as the captain could make himself heard he asked Jim how it had fared with him. Jim said he had almost had enough of it.

"In another hour you will be able to free yourself," returned the captain.

In less than that time the sea had ceased to break dangerously over the Lapwing, and after waiting a while the captain cast loose the bonds that held them to the wheel.

"You may go down below now," he said, "and get a bottle of brandy. A good drink won't hurt us."

Jim was stiff and sore, but he managed to crawl to the companion, open it, and go below.

He had no difficulty in finding a bottle of brandy, for he knew where the old captain kept his store.

With a bottle in one hand and a drinking-cup in his pocket he crept back to the deck.

Captain Broadman took the bottle, fished his jack-knife out of his pocket, and with a dexterous tap of the blade broke the neck off just where the body of the bottle began.

"It is not a time for corkscrews, my lad," he said. "Drink—don't be afraid of it for once. Brandy is a bad beverage but a good stimulant in the time of trouble."

Jim drank half a tumbler of brandy—more than he had ever swallowed at a single sitting or standing before—and it gave him back new life.

The captain, for his share, partook of a whole tumblerful.

It was not until they had temporarily restored themselves that they spoke of what they had recently endured, and, like brave men, each confessed that more than once they had given themselves up for lost.

"There was one wave I fancied would pound us into matchwood," remarked the captain. "I felt it curl over us, shutting out the air, and, although it couldn't have been more than a moment or two before it fell upon us like an avalanche, I thought of many things."

"Twice," said Jim, "I believed I should not get

back my breath, and I tried to pray, but the words would not come."

"Prayer," observed the captain, sententiously, "isn't a thing you can take up properly now and again. It's got to be a matter of habit, or you will bungle it."

A steady breeze was still blowing, but with their bit of canvas gone they knew they could make little headway before it.

"To-morrow," said the captain, "we will put up a fresh sail."

After a time he persuaded Jim to go down and get a little sleep, so the youth, feeling more worn out than he had ever done before, crept below, and, tumbling into the captain's bunk, was instantly asleep.

CHAPTER XV.

THE ISLAND—JIM GOES ON A PERILOUS JOURNEY— A TIME OF ANXIETY.

Y AND BYE, after many hours, Jim opened his eyes, and in a lazy, self-satisfied way tried to make out where he was.

By degrees the events of the previous night came back to him, and, sitting up, he stared about the cabin, and saw that it was broad daylight—

" I've been asleep half the day," he said, as he tumbled out.

As he had slept in his clothes he had no toilet to make, and, feeling his old elasticity had returned, he bounded up to the deck.

His first thought was to look for the captain, and there he was, leaning over the bows, smoking his pipe and staring at a line of tremendous cliffs, not more than two furlongs ahead, towards which the ship was drifting with the tide.

As Jim advanced he heard his foostep and turned. His face, strange to say, was radiant.

" Jim, my lad," he said, " I must have been out in my reckoning. We are *there*."

To this Jim, not knowing what " there " might mean, could only say he was glad to hear it.

" There," repeated the captain, " but on the wrong side of the island. That won't matter so very much, provided we can find a way up that wall," pointing to the cliffs, " but I'm bound to say it don't look over promising."

" We will get up somehow," said Jim.

They were moving pretty freely under a strong tide, and would presently ground against the foot of the cliffs.

They knew the water was shallow, by the breakers, and there was a thin line of beach still visible.

" It's nigh high-tide," said the captain, " and we shall ground beautifully. Then our first duty must be to anchor the Lapwing, so that she won't be dragged away again."

Jim joined the captain at the bows, and in silence they watched the gradual approach, the cliff

myriads of sea-birds flying up and down the face
of it.

It was the most inspiring spectacle Jim had ever
seen, and the prospect of climbing the tremendous
elevation did not appear to be very great.

But he remembered the old motto "Where
there's a will there's a way," and gathered heart.

Drawing nearer, he could make out little irregu-
larities on the wall-like cliff which promised a foothold, and the captain, finding tongue again, pointed
out ledges where the sea-birds had laid their nests,
and called them resting-places.

"One of us must go first," he said, "and take
a cord with him. After the cord a rope can be
pulled up, and once a rope is secured above it's a
poor sailor who can't make it a staircase."

"I will go first," answered Jim. "But why have
you allowed me to sleep so long? It must be near
noon."

"When we are going to take a horse on a tough
journey, what do we do?" asked the captain.
"Why, rest him well. At dawn to-day I saw the
island, and knew what had to be done. The lad
to lead the way was below sleeping, and I let him
sleep. After sleep he wants something to eat. Sit
down and I will get your breakfast. I had mine
five hours ago."

Jim demurred to being waited on, but the captain
insisted upon the arrangement, and breakfast was
soon ready.

While Jim was partaking of it the old captain
brought up from the store-room a dozen balls of
stout twine and fastened the ends together, ready
for their being paid out when Jim began to scale the
cliff.

He also brought out a small axe and a couple of hooks, the latter for Jim to use as a help in holding on where the way was most dangerous.

"Sling 'em round your neck," said the captain, "and use 'em when you want 'em."

The end of the twine was put round Jim's waist and knotted behind, so as not to impede his movements, and as soon as the Lapwing was well aground he dropped down over her side and waded up to the foot of the cliff.

"I shall be busy, too," sung out the captain, "and not worriting myself by watching you. Go steady, eyes up, and a firm grip—try every place as you go."

"Aye! aye," cried Jim.

On a closer inspection he found the face of the cliff more rugged than he had hoped for. At the base, at least, there was a fairly good foot and hand hold.

With set teeth and a strong will to get to the top of the cliff, whatever might be the perils of the way, he began his journey.

Captain Broadman watched him for a few minutes, and then, with a pleasant smile upon his face, he began his own task.

The first thing he did was to get up a spare top-mast and saw it in two. The pieces he tossed ashore out of the reach of the tide.

Then he fetched a huge wooden mallet, known in some parts of England as a beadel, which he tossed in the same direction.

After this he uncoiled several yards of a spare anchor hawser and dropped the end of it overboard.

Last of all he lowered the rope-ladder which had

done such good service before, and descended to the beach.

His next care was to find a spot close by where the two pieces of topmast could be driven in stake-fashion, at an angle that would allow of their being holdfasts for the hawser, his purpose being to secure the Lapwing against any possible chance of being floated off with the tide.

That there would be a possibility of this he knew, for it was his intention, as soon as Jim had got a rope on the summit of the cliff, to get a pulley fixed there and run up the most precious part of the cargo—in his eyes—the cases of arms and the dynamite.

He had perfect faith in Jim's successfully performing the task allotted him, and it was his intention to avoid even so much as looking up at him until he heard from aloft the cry announcing success.

But he could not carry out this resolve. Curiosity and anxiety were a little too much for him.

Therefore, when he had driven in one stake, he was impelled to step out far enough into the water to see what Jim was doing.

Already he had made good headway, and was nearly a hundred feet up, presenting the appearance of progressing fly-fashion, with suckers on his hands and feet.

The delicate twine suspended from Jim's waist was blown out, and by the additional length thereby unrolled conveyed a wonderfully impressive idea of the height he had already attained.

"He's a bold lad," muttered the captain, "and Heaven help him to the top."

stake—sloping, as the other did, towards the cliff. Then he had another look at Jim.

He was higher now, and was little more than a black patch against the cliff. He was moving very slowly and cautiously, feeling his way.

"I can't look again," muttered the old seaman.

Nor could he go on with his work, for he was trembling for Jim's safety.

If anything happened to him the old captain would be left alone, for where the Lapwing had grounded was in the centre of a semi-circle of cliff, the two ends of which were, undoubtedly, always in deep water.

The road Jim was taking was the only way up to the interior of the island.

Seating himself upon the sand close up against the cliff, the captain pulled out his watch and laid it down beside him.

"I'll give him five minutes," he said. "He ought to be at the top by that time."

He shut his eyes, and kept them tightly closed until he thought the five minutes had elapsed. Then he opened them again.

His watch showed that barely a minute of the time had passed away.

"It must be stopped," he muttered.

But the tick-tick of the good, old-fashioned chronometer could be plainly heard, and he had to shut his eyes again. He tried to think of anything except the youth in his perilous position, but in spite of his efforts to distract his thoughts he pictured him every few minutes as slipping and falling.

rose high above the screaming of the sea-birds soaring to and fro.

With a start he opened his eyes, and stared up and down and round about him, fearing to see the form of Jim lying huddled up—smashed by the dreadful fall.

But as yet all was well.

Then he pictured to himself Jim coming to a part of the cliff which would shut out all hopes of going a foot higher, and what then would be his fate?

He could not return by the way he came—the steep cliff forbade that—and then the youth would be unable to go up or down—fixed to an insecure spot, with the certainty of ultimate death before him.

He could see the twine bellying out before the breeze, and as he gazed at it there was no sign of its being drawn out further.

Surely Jim had been brought to a full stop, as he feared.

"His death will be on my head!" groaned the captain. "I am a man accursed."

He buried his face in his hands and sat still for a little while, quite overcome with the emotion within him.

It was not so much of himself he thought as of the youth, who, in his feverish fancy, appeared to him to be doomed.

The life they had recently led together had endeared Jim to the old seaman, and he had learnt to love him as a son, but he never knew how dear he had become to him until then.

"It was for me to scale the cliff," he groaned,

had come to an end. I've had a bit of a fling in my time, but he as yet has only begun to taste life."

He would have given all he had and hoped for in this world to see Jim standing before him in the full possession of his health and strength, and if a word could have brought him back it would have been cheerfully spoken. But it could not be.

He looked once more at the twine. It was again paying out.

Presently the last ball of it slipped over the side of the vessel and fell into the shallow water eddying round the Lapwing.

There it danced about as it unwound, and with a feeling of intense relief the watching man realised that Jim was still going up.

Suddenly the ball ceased to roll about, and a portion of the loosened twine fell into the sea.

What did that mean?

There was a catching in the breath of the captain, and he sprang to his feet.

A rushing sound above fell upon his ears.

A heavy body was coming to the ground.

He heard it bump here and there, and then, as he closed his eyes and staggered back, it fell with a sickening thud at his feet.

CHAPTER XVI.

NOT DEAD YET—THE WORK OF CLEARING THE SHIP— ANOTHER PERILOUS ASCENT.

 TANDING dumb and still with fear the unhappy Captain Broadman listened for some faint moan to assure him that Jim, whom he believed had fallen from the cliff, was yet alive.

But there was not a sound.

At length with dread he opened his eyes, and looked about for the contused and mangled form he had been picturing in his mind's eye—but it was not there.

Hard by there was a large stone and a mass of loose earth, which had fallen from above, and that was all.

The revulsion from intense grief to hope and joy was almost as painful as the shock he had received, but bracing himself against it he stepped out, and shading his eyes with his hand looked up the cliff.

Jim was there, just clambering over the topmost edge, having performed the dangerous ascent in safety.

"Hurrah! my lad," roared the old captain.

Jim looked down and waved his hand by way of reply.

Then he began to haul in the twine, which the light-hearted old seaman below attached the finer rope to.

They had plenty of material to work with and

within an hour the stouter rope was well secured aloft and hung quiescent, too heavy for the wind to stir against the face of the cliff.

Jim was soon busy, Having secured the anchor rope he lowered the lighter one again, and to this the captain attached a pulley and a spar. With this Jim fixed up a hoisting apparatus, and then the business of getting stores aloft began.

First of all provisions were sent up for Jim's use, and after that a blanket to sleep on, for the two men were to be separated for a while.

For Jim to attempt to return and the captain to scale the cliff would be a waste of time and energy.

They worked on, with brief spells of rest, until sundown, and with the aid of the running rope and pulley a considerable quantity of the lighter stores were got aloft.

Once the captain wrote and sent above the following message, written on a slip of paper, with a pencil attached to it—

" *Do you see any signs of men about ?*"

To which came back the reply—

" *Nothing but a splendid country—quite a garden.*"

One more message was sent up just as it was getting dark—

" *Good-night, dear lad. Make a bit of a shelter to sleep in ; the dew is sure to be heavy.*"

Jim sent back another good-night, and then each went to rest in his allotted place.

The captain, of course, slept on board, and Jim constructed a rough kind of tent, under which he was far more comfortable than he would have been in a stuffy house.

They were up with the sun, and having exchanged a cheery salute partook of breakfast.

After that the toil of the day began.

Everything that could be of the least service to them on the island was to be taken out of the ship, and only the bare hulk of the Lapwing left.

There was little chance of the staunch old ship ever being of any use to them again.

Another day passed, in which a really extraordinary amount of work was done. Every hour or so some message or cheery word was exchanged.

Jim said it was "the jolliest thing" he had ever had to do with. He was enjoying himself immensely.

Thus for three days they lived and laboured asunder, the last packages sent up being those comprising arms and explosives, and the captain, for obvious reasons, took especial care to firmly secure them ere they were launched upon their upward journey.

At length everything had been sent aloft without an approach to an accident, thanks to the manner in which the work had been done.

Last of all there was the captain himself to be transported to the summit of the cliff.

His heart was stout, but he knew that neither eye nor hand were what they had been, and he was not ashamed to get assistance from Jim.

Having attached the smaller rope to his waist, he instructed Jim to haul up gently, so as to keep it just taut. If he slipped it would be the means of saving him from a fall.

Then he began the ascent.

Jim's track was clear, and the captain knew he could not do better than follow it. As he slowly felt his way he saw for the first time the full nature of the perils his young friend had passed

Had he attempted the ascent without the aid of the rope he must have failed, for he lost his footing a dozen times, but the friendly rope saved him.

Jim, watching aloft, took good care that it should be always taut, or nearly so, and he had given it a turn round a stake in the ground, which prevented it from slipping.

After he had slipped the old seaman sometimes swung to and fro several times before he could regain a foothold.

It would have been too much for a man of weak nerves, but the gallant sailor kept cool, and, having got another start, continued his ascent.

At length the summit was reached, and Jim gave him a hand to help him over the edge of it.

Safe and unharmed, the old seaman held that hand fast, and, kneeling, remained still for a few moments with his head upon his breast.

"It's right and manful," he said, as he rose to his feet, "to bear the ills of life with resignation and to be humbly thankful for its mercies."

What a strange sight it was on the summit of that cliff.

Arranged in different heaps were the stores of the ship, all classified as carefully as if a ship's purser had superintended the arrangement.

The old captain cast his eye around and bestowed upon Jim an appreciative pat on the back.

"Jim, my dear boy," he said, "you are the right stuff all through. You would have made your mark anywhere."

"I am afraid I was not making much of a mark at home," replied Jim, with a light laugh—"at least

"It doesn't matter," answered Jim, with a sigh. "I shall never see them again."

"Oh! but you will," rejoined the old seaman, cheerily, "when you return with a ship laden with stuff as good as gold."

"In that case," said Jim, grimly, "the ship would get the welcome."

"Well, my lad," replied the captain, "I don't want to pry into your affairs, but for all that one of these days, when you've a mind to speak, I should like to know your history."

"Oh! there isn't much to tell," said Jim. "I'm not the runaway son of a duke, nor am I heir to a title or estate. And now, Captain Broadman, what are we to do next?"

"Rest to-day, and to-morrow take a run across the island," replied the old seaman. "Over there," extending his arm across the island, "I ought to find my friends."

"Are they far away?"

"I can't tell the exact distance, my lad, but I should say seven or eight miles—right through yonder wood—and there's no road that I know of."

Among the things they had brought from the ship were rolls of canvas and cloth and spare sails, some of which were utilised in covering up the stores that might suffer from the sun and possible rain.

As the wind blew pretty fresh at that elevation these coverings had to be securely pegged to the ground to prevent their being blown away.

This occupied the time while daylight lasted, and when at last they laid down on the lee side of a pile of packing-cases to rest, the sleep they wooed came.

CHAPTER XVII.

THE ISLAND—WHERE ARE THE CAPTAIN'S FRIENDS?—
A DESERTED STATION.

IM dreamt of a battle-field and of big guns firing. When he awoke he found that the wind was responsible for the suggestion. Quite a gale was blowing.

The canvas coverings were swelling up with the air that got under them, and here and there a corner had got loose, so they went to work to make them additionally secure.

Heavy stones were laid upon the top and tent-pegs driven into the ground.

That done they secured the arms and provisions which they had laid aside the previous night for the excursion, and started off with their heads to the gale.

From the cliff the land inwards sloped rapidly down to a wood, where they lost the pressure of the breeze and found themselves in comparative calm.

Wood dry and ready to burn abounded, and they soon had a fire burning, beside which they partook of breakfast.

The old seaman was thoughtful during the meal, and Jim was wondering what he had on his mind when he suddenly blurted out—

" It's odd, anyway—not even so much as the sign of a fire."

" Where ?" asked Jim.

" Why, anywhere on the island," said the captain.

"I aint said much about it, but ever since noon yesterday a dreadful thought has laid hold of me."

"Whatever it is let me share it," suggested Jim, earnestly.

"It's this, my lad," replied the captain, "it's just possible—I don't say it is so, mind—just possible *that we've got upon the wrong island after all!*"

"Well, we won't trouble about that," returned Jim, cheerfully. "As far as the right one goes I know nothing about it, and I shall not miss much."

"But I shall," said the old seaman, and a haggard expression came over his face. "You see, I was the discoverer of it—"

He stopped short, and Jim kept quiet, hoping he would let him know what "it" was.

But the captain said no more.

He had finished his breakfast of tinned meat and biscuit, and shutting his clasp-knife he rose to his feet.

"Will it be safe to leave the fire here?" asked Jim.

"No, lad," replied the captain; "spread it out and tread it under. Some of it might be blown up yonder, and the wood being dry it's likely to catch alight. Get it all out, and then we will go on."

He filled his pipe, and after a whiff or two his cheerful condition returned.

"It's all right, my lad," he said; "this *is* the island. There can't be two exactly alike in the world. If there is I never heard of 'em."

Jim put out the fire, packed up the things, and slung the bundle on his back. They were armed

As the wood stretched for a considerable distance to the right and left they decided to strike through it.

The undergrowth was rather thick, but it was not thorny, and could be easily broken through or trodden underfoot.

"Go easy, my lad," said the captain; "there may be snakes, and a bite would be awkward."

It was such a wood or forest as Jim had never seen before. Some of the trees were huge, with trunks thirty or forty feet in diameter, rising up bare and straight sixty or seventy feet ere a branch spread out.

Others were slender, some were gnarled, and here and there one grew in twisted form, so as to have a rugged resemblance to a corkscrew.

The majority of the trees were strange even to the captain. He pointed out the mimosa and a species of palm, but the greater part were, as he admitted, unknown to him.

"Many of these trees have iron insides," he said, "just as if they were being slowly petrified from the centre. I've got my theory for that, which scientific men would laugh at. They always laugh at what they don't know and cannot understand."

An hour was occupied in getting through the wood to the more open country beyond.

Here they found a broad and fertile plain, with a line of hills resembling the billows of the sea in the distance.

Scattered about were trees which were laden with varieties of the pear and plum. These they tried and

In proof of what he said he pointed to branches where the fruit, in every stage of development, from the blossom to the full-grown pear or plum, could be seen.

Trailing about the ground, and also laden with fruit, were vines bearing grapes about as fine and quite as well-flavoured as the production of our best hothouses at home. Jim was very fond of grapes, and he would have eaten very liberally of them but for the captain, who bade him be careful at first, lest, after so long an abstention from that class of food, he might make himself ill.

The prospect all round was cheering.

In any case they were not likely to starve on the island, for in their progress they met a great variety of game, including a species of wild hog, and partridges, or what looked like them, abounded.

When the base of the hills was reached they halted for another rest, and slept awhile in a shady spot during the heat of the day.

As soon as the afternoon was well advanced they pursued their journey, and an hour's steady climbing brought them to the summit of the hills, which commanded a view of the sea on the other side of the island.

But intervening there was another track of comparatively level ground, which the captain scanned closely, and presently took off his cap and waved it aloft.

"All right, my lad," he cried, "it's OUR island."

Under his guiding finger Jim was able to make out a variety of huts dotted about near the coast. They varied in size, some being of modest dimensions, and three of considerable length, which the captain said were "workshops."

"It is there," he said, "we shall find our friends."

"I do not see any people moving about," remarked Jim.

"No," answered the captain, with a somewhat troubled air; "but perhaps they are resting or experimenting. It's all right, my lad, we're THERE."

He was now in feverish haste to get on, showing more nervous anxiety than he had before exhibited in Jim's presence. The slope of the hill was easy travelling, and they hurried forward.

Ere they had travelled far on the level ground they came to a log hut, the door of which stood open, and the captain shouted to give the inmates notice of his coming.

But there was no response, and when they had reached the door of the hut they found the place empty.

Inside there was some rugged furniture and fittings, such as squatters consider sufficient for their wants, and there were signs of recent occupation, but naught in the way of life.

"It is nothing but what I might expect," said the captain; "he's down with the others."

He tried to put a good face on the matter, but was undoubtedly troubled. In silence he pursued his way to another hut, and that was empty too.

So on he went from hut to hut, with the readiness of a man familiar with the ground, and the result was the same.

The last visit was to one of the larger buildings, which proved to be a species of workshop, for inside it were benches and seats for workmen, and at the far end was an iron furnace of the class used for the smelting of metals. The now dismayed captain walked up to it and laid his hand upon the furnace.

"Not *quite* cold," he muttered. "Then they can't be far away."

He sat down upon a low stool, his face resting on his hands, and so remained for a while thinking. At length he looked up, and Jim saw that his face was haggard and worn, as if he had just gone through a weary night of it.

"I don't see any reason why they have deserted the place," he said, "can you, my lad?"

"I don't even know who THEY are," replied Jim.

"Oh! I forgot," muttered the captain. "They were friends of mine, and promised to remain here until I came back. It's odd they should have gone."

"Perhaps they gave you up," suggested Jim; "they expected you earlier."

"Yes—yes, it may be that," replied the old seaman, "but I'm not more than three weeks behind, anyway, and they need not have been in such a hurry to go."

He got up, and, motioning to Jim to follow him, walked slowly from the building. He said nothing more just then, but after a little undecided pacing to and fro he faced about and walked across a patch of ground strewn with broken pieces of rock and a coarse kind of grass growing between.

He did not hesitate, but pushed open the door of another small hut and entered.

"We'll take up our quarters here," he said, "and wait until the morning. Mayhap they have gone out hunting."

"Hunting!" thought Jim; "it's odd if they are. But the whole thing is odd, and there's an end of it."

"We will wait until to-morrow," said the captain, "and then, if they don't return, I'll set to work—

you and I, my lad. Till then don't ask me what it all means, for I'm a bit disturbed now."

He said little more, but during the hours between their arrival and sunset moved uneasily about in and out of the hut, looking about him and listening for the men who had so strangely vanished.

"The marvel of it is," Jim heard him mutter, "that they couldn't have been gone an hour when I sighted the place, so *how did they get away ?*"

Thus he kept on at intervals, and Jim was as nearly eaten up with curiosity as a young fellow can be. But he killed the time and distracted his thoughts by arranging two beds with some blankets he found in the hut, and preparing supper with the remaining portion of food they had brought with them.

By and bye they turned in, but not, as far as the captain was concerned, to sleep.

Long after Jim was dreaming, unconscious of anything around him, the old seaman at intervals sat up to listen or rose and went to the door to let in the persons who never came.

There was a cool breeze blowing which was grateful in the natural heat of the climate, and it was the rustling of trees that misled the watchful man.

Many hours were passed, and the night was almost spent when he at length slept also, forgetful of his troubles and anxieties, whatever their nature might be.

When Jim awoke it was daylight, and seeing that his companion was soundly sleeping he got up and went softly out of the hut.

The sun had risen about an hour and the wind had gone down. The air was still, and there was promise

THE GUN BELCHED FORTH, AND A LINE OF IRON STRUCK THE SAVAGE HORDE WELL IN THE CENTRE.

Jim thought he would take a look round to see if he could find out the nature of the occupation of the men who had vanished from the place.

His search was soon, in a measure, rewarded by his coming across a spot where digging had been going on.

The spade was there, as it had been thrown aside by the hand that had been using it.

No great amount of work had been done. The hole was only a few feet in diameter and three or four deep, but below the surface it was the strangest soil Jim had ever seen.

Taking some in his hand he found it was very heavy, and on examining it closely discovered that it was permeated with metallic particles, but the nature of that metal was not clear.

While thus engaged a slight exclamation from someone near reached his ear.

Raising his eyes, he was startled by the sight of a swarthy savage, armed with spear and shield, approaching him.

The manner of the man indicated determined hostility, and Jim clapped his hand to his side in search of his revolver.

But he had left it behind in the hut, and he was practically unarmed and defenceless.

CHAPTER XVIII.

DODGING A BULLET—THE DEAD MAWATTA AND HIS CANOE—PREPARING FOR TROUBLOUS TIMES TO COME.

ITH upraised arm—poising the spear so as to take sure aim at Jim—the savage stood, and then he hurled it, but not with the precision he intended, for as the weapon was about to leave his hand a shout from Captain Broadman disturbed him.

It was only by an inch or two that it missed its mark, but a miss is as good as a mile, according to the old proverb, and Jim was saved so far.

At the same moment a wiry hound, which Jim had hitherto not seen, sprang upon him. He gave it a violent kick and it fell back howling.

The agile savage turned in the direction of the captain, who had emerged from the hut in the nick of time, rifle in hand, and was now taking aim at the dog, which he shot with one barrel, and turned his attention to the swarthy foe.

Then Jim saw an extraordinary scene, in which the savage and the old captain were the actors.

The former, instead of running away, as one might have expected, seemed to think that it would be useless to do so, or it might be that he was unwilling to exhibit cowardice, for instead of hurrying off he began to dance this way and that, throwing himself upon the ground, bounding up again, and going through a series of movements of such a rapid nature that it was difficult for the eye to follow him.

His intention was pretty clear. He knew the use of a gun, and was doing his best to dodge the bullet.

Captain Broadman was in no hurry.

Slowly advancing, he kept his weapon at the present, biding his time until the wild antics of the savage should cease. Gymnastics so exhausting could not be long continued, and presently the wild performer's energies began to flag.

As he rose from a roll upon the ground he remained one moment erect and motionless, and that was fatal to him.

A sharp report rang out, and he leaped into the air like a merino sheep, pitched forward on his head, and lay still.

"Don't touch him yet," shouted Captain Broadman, as Jim was advancing toward the fallen foe. "You can't trust the breed."

He hurried up, replacing the exploded cartridge with a fresh one as he came, and, halting within two or three yards of the body, looked it carefully over.

"I've hit him," he said to Jim, "for he is bleeding. I'll cover him while you turn him over."

Jim laid hold of the arm of the savage and turned him face upward. All doubts were then set at rest. He was dead.

On his breast there was a small round hole, from which the blood was slowly oozing. The aim of the old seaman had been so true that the leaden missile had gone straight to his heart.

"If I hadn't known him to have been one of a tribe the most cruel and bloodthirsty on earth," said the captain, "I might have spared him; but it's useless to show mercy to a Mawatta. It is a thing they have never practised, and don't understand."

"I did not know there were any such people here," returned Jim.

"Nor I," answered the captain, with a troubled face. "The home of the Mawattas, is on an island twenty miles from here, and I had no idea they voyaged so far. I understand the huts being empty now. Well, devil's dog as he is, let us give him burial."

The hole which Jim had been inspecting, with a little lengthening, served the purpose of a grave, and having laid the body there and covered it over, the two men returned to the hut.

"I'll not conceal from you, my lad," said the captain, "that I was not prepared to meet a foe—I thought of friends only—and they have been cruelly murdered and *eaten*, for the Mawatta is a cannibal. There is one chance for us. He may have been left here alone, or came by himself across the sea after the main body had returned—but we can't trust to that."

"How many friends had you here?" asked Jim.

"A dozen, good men and true," answered the captain, "officers and seamen I've had under me. They must have been taken by surprise in the night, I guess, and bound and carried away ere they had time to defend themselves. It's a horrible thought. What tortures they must have suffered. Poor fellows!

"But all the grieving in the world," he added, "won't help them or us. What we have to do is to be prepared to defend ourselves, and the stores on the cliff have to be got here *somehow*. We will begin to-day."

After breakfast Jim, at the suggestion of the captain, climbed a tree close by, and from its summit took a survey of the island.

He could see no trace of any others of the Mawatta tribe in sight, but made out a small speck, boat-shaped, on the shore about a mile away.

This, in the captain's opinion, was good tidings, for it pointed to the conclusion that the savage had come alone, and to make sure he and Jim, armed with all the weapons they had, journeyed to the shore and walked along it until they came to a lone canoe.

It had no paddle, but the captain explained that the Mawatta, with instinctive cunning, had hidden it away to prevent his boat being stolen.

There was little doubt that he had come alone.

The canoe was made of bark of a thick, leathery nature, shaped and bound, or rather stitched together, with leathern thongs of untanned hide.

It was about twelve feet long and would hold three persons, for whom seats had been fixed.

"Is it possible that this frail thing can be piloted across the sea?" inquired Jim.

"These craft," explained the captain, "are wonderfully buoyant. The Mawatta is skilful with his paddle, and this latitude is favoured with long and regular spells of calm weather. The stormy seasons are short, and come round as regular as clockwork. Still, I've never seen or heard of a Mawatta so far from home."

"You have visited their island, I suppose?" suggested Jim.

"I've been past it twice," returned the captain, with a dry smile, "but I knew its character, and didn't land, although invited by the treacherous beggars with friendly signs. No visitors rash enough to go ashore, unless numerous and well armed, ever return alive."

"Would it not be possible to exterminate the race?" asked Jim.

"It would," said the captain, "if you could get at them, but it would take a small army to do it, for the Mawatta Island is high and rugged, and there are places almost inaccessible except to men as active as cats, while the crafty natives have a thousand hiding-places. The island is remote from the ordinary track of vessels, and no nation has thought it worth while to annex it. But even that will be done some day. The savage is bound to go."

They were hovering round the canoe while talking, the captain having something on his mind concerning it, which he now laid before Jim.

"My lad," he said, "this canoe may be useful some day. We had better take it back with us and hide it somewhere. It's light enough—a strong boy could carry it—and one day, when we have nothing better to do, we will come and have a hunt for the paddle."

They took up the canoe between them and carried it back, without finding it much of a burden.

In the heart of a small grove of trees they hollowed out a hiding-place for it, just deep enough for it to be sunk out of sight, finally covering it lightly with earth, and marking the spot by notching the bark of two of the trees.

That done, they set out again for the cliff on the other side of the island, to begin the arduous task of removing their stores to the log hut which they proposed to make their abode.

"It'll be a long job," said the captain—"a matter

of weeks—but it's better than idling about. Situated as we are, we don't want too much time to *think*."

"And should the main body of Mawattas come again?" hinted Jim.

"When they do," replied the captain, "I hope to be prepared for them."

They had not inspected all the huts, for that was needless, but in one of them was a collection of material which the captain spoke of as being possibly useful by and bye.

"I daresay the wretches stole all they could carry," said the captain, with a laugh, "but there was one thing that would puzzle 'em to take."

"What is that?" asked Jim.

"A small field-gun—a cannon," answered the captain. "It was brought here last voyage, to be a defence against possible foes—that were *not* savage. It's packed in pieces, but I can put it together—and there's ammunition for it, too. But first of all our own stores must be got across the island. After that we can have a look around to see what is left of the old lot."

CHAPTER XIX.

THE STORES REMOVED—A CHANGE OF SEASON—THE STORY OF THE ISLAND—ITS GREAT WEALTH.

IME flies swiftly with busy men, and a whole month passed rapidly by without Jim 'experiencing anything like the *ennui* which might have arisen from his semi-solitary life upon the island.

One thing added greatly to their labours—the necessity for breaking up the larger packages and making parcels of their contents convenient for transportation.

But the work was done at last—and well done—without any hindrance.

The weather favoured them, and the Mawattas did not put in an appearance.

The whole of the stores were ranged round the end of the long hut, and the next thing to do was to put up some sort of screen to save them from the chance of being set alight by a spark from the fire, which they might have occasionally to light in the hut.

A portion of the materials of one of the adjoining huts was employed in the erection of a partition, which not only shielded the stores, but gave a snugness to that part of the hut set apart for habitation.

As a security against intrusion or attack an open window in the store was securely fastened up, and a shutter made for a similar orifice in the inhabited portion of the hut.

Of the stores which had been in possession of the captain's friends very little remained.

The Mawattas, the assumed despoilers, had taken away everything portable, even to clothes.

But three strong chests had defied their efforts to open them and had proved too heavy to bear away.

These were lodged in a hut that stood quite alone, about two hundred yards away, and Captain Broadman explained that it had been occupied by a mechanical engineer named Watts, who had been appointed to fix together the cannon the three cases contained.

"But he never had the chance of doing it, poor fellow," sighed the old seaman; "such a likely young fellow, too. It makes me mad to think of his being EATEN."

It was the captain's intention to open the cases the day after the arduous task of removing the stores had been completed, but as both had need of rest he postponed the task for twenty-four hours.

That very night one of the periodical rough stormy seasons set in.

Shortly after sunset the wind suddenly rose and blew almost a hurricane. Thunder, and lightning, and rain shortly followed.

These outbursts of nature generally lasted about a week, sunshine and storm alternating with wonderful rapidity.

"It isn't safe to go abroad for an hour," the captain said, "unless you are hungering for a soaking. The best place for the time is under shelter."

They had plenty of indoor work at hand, for it is

instinctive in civilised man to do his best to make the humblest home comfortable.

There were boxes of tools to look over—and in some cases clean and sharpen—hammocks to be slung, cooking utensils to clean and arrange.

All the arms also wanted overhauling, and, last of all, there was the cooking, which the two men shared between them.

This was the work of the day, and at night they sat by the small wood fire, kept burning "for company's sake," listening to the swirl of the rain, the roaring of the wind, and the booming of the thunder.

In the quieter intervals they talked, and it was during one of these lulls that the captain opened his heart at last about the island.

"Perhaps I ought not to have made a secret of it," he said ; "and I didn't do so because I could not trust you, but I feared it would unsettle you for useful work. My lad, we are living on a wealth of metal such as the world has never heard of nor seen before."

He stopped for a moment to light his pipe, and bade Jim smoke also, as it had a soothing effect.

"It is now seven years ago," he began, "that I first lighted on this island. I was commanding the Swordfish, trading in fruit and such like, which I used to fetch from places where things could be had almost for the asking. I got into a storm that partly disabled the ship and drove us out of our course. We were not wrecked, but when the calm weather came, as it always does for a day or two after the storms, we were close to this island, and we anchored to get water and do some repairs.

"As we were bound to lie here for about a week, I

spent—like the rest of the crew—as much time as I
could spare on shore, and it was while rambling
about in search of something to shoot that I came
across a very strange thing—nothing to alarm a
man, but out and out surprising. It was what
looked to be a big copper boiler turned upside down
and buried in the earth.

"A boiler here!" exclaimed Jim.

"No, it wasn't that—it only looked like it,"
continued the captain. "It was something better,
being nothing more or less than the crown of a
solid metal HILL, which at one time must have
stood up bare, but in the course of centuries had
got almost buried by the earth that gets on to every
new island from goodness knows where. Vegetation
follows the earth, and there's your fertile island.

"It was a staggerer to me," pursued the captain,
"but, mind you, I didn't know at first it was the
crown of a hill—that I was told of afterwards.
All I could make out was that it was *solid*. Now I
had on board the ship a scientific gentleman named
Drew, who had come on a voyage for his health
and to amuse himself, whenever he got a chance,
by finding out something new about this wonderful
world. I told him what I had discovered, and he
came to see it. Well, from that place we went
here and there, making out, what I believe to be
true, that this island is the richest spot on earth in
all metals save one, and that is gold.

"But Drew said to me, 'Never mind there being
no gold. You have silver and copper and tin, and
some of the rarest metals known; but you must
confide it only to a few friends to work it with you,
or you will have all the world rushing here.' You
see what he was driving at, Jim?"

"Yes, I do," answered Jim.   "After all, it isn't your island, and any other man would have as great a right as you here."

"Right, my lad," rejoined the old seaman. "Then came the conviction that I could do nothing alone. A thousand men, in the ordinary way, could not carry on the mining of this island, and, of course, Jack would be as good as his master. Drew and I talked it over, and I assisted him to a solution of the trouble.   Here's the things he proposed."

Holding up his left hand, the fingers spread out, the captain ticked off with his right the following list of proposals made by Drew—

"A private company to be formed, to consist of not more than a score of persons.

"To arrange with them to live on the island for a term of years, working and smelting the metals until there was a fortune for each.

"To secure a ship for the conveyance of materials for work, necessaries of life, and arms for defence against intruders.

"The penalty of revealing the secret to anyone not included in the company to be death.

"It was necessary to be strict, my lad," said the narrator, resuming his ordinary manner, "or the whole thing would be ruined. It was Drew who told me dynamite, properly used, would do more work in a day than a hundred men would in a month, and he invented a special drilling-machine, which promised to do wonders, but that's been broken up and carried away by the Mawattas."

"Was Drew one of the men on the island?" asked Jim.

"Yes, poor fellow !" was the answer. "He threw his whole soul into the work, and it did him good.

After we got home—in the Swordfish—it was his money that bought the Lapwing, and we went out first with a few trusty men and a cargo suited to our purpose. It was stowed away in a hut—just as this lot is now—and by some mischance caught fire."

"What! the dynamite?" exclaimed Jim.

"Yes," answered the captain, "and a big flare it was, but no explosion to speak of. Dynamite will burn without doing much harm. It is when there is *concussion* that the mischief comes in."

"I was not aware of that," said Jim.

"Well, the stores were destroyed," resumed the captain, "and I had to come back to England for another cargo. Brown accompanied me—the vessel being manned by a shipwrecked crew we had rescued from that side of the island where we landed, and whom we were glad to pay off directly we got into dock. We were soon loaded. Of the trouble we had to get another crew you know, also all that followed."

"But suppose you had arrived here safely with that lot of rascals," said Jim, "how would you have acted?"

"They would have been allowed—at least, all who were trustworthy—to join us," said the old seaman. "A rascal or two could easily have been dealt with, but I did not expect the whole lot would be black."

"Perhaps you were in too much hurry to get a crew?" suggested Jim.

"I was," frankly replied the captain. "You see, time was flying, and I am not so young as I was. When a man gets' the wrong side of fifty he can't dally. It was a mistake, but it can't be helped now, Jim. You and I are here alone to do the best we can.   We can only work and hope.   There's wealth enough here to make us richer than any monarch who ever sat upon a throne."

" After it has been got out of the ground," thought Jim.

Here the storm broke ·out afresh, and the hour being late the two lone men went to rest.

CHAPTER XX.

THE RETURN OF FINE WEATHER—THE MAWATTAS ARRIVE—THE ATTACK ON THE HUT—A TERRIBLE BOMB.

JIM could not sleep at first, for the story of the captain haunted him. It was not totally different to what he expected, for he had, at intervals, thought over what he discovered of the nature of the sub-soil, but he was not so sanguine as the captain was about results.

Suppose they laboured, and dug or blasted from the hard ground the wealth of a kingdom, what would it avail them if they fell victims to the Mawattas or had no chance of being rescued ?

Again, suppose a ship did come near and take them off, would not their wealth have to be left behind them ?

It seemed to be a puzzling, harassing affair, more

difficult than most things of being solved with satisfaction.

"Had it been a matter of ordinary hidden treasure," thought Jim, "it would be different. But— Well, there, I won't bother about it."

And determined not to do so he shut his eyes, thought of home, and fell asleep.

The next day was stormy, and the next, and often during the times of leisure the prospects of the future were discussed.

The ideas of the old captain were feasible. It was his plan that they should look out a suitable hiding-place, where they could store away any metal they might be able to reclaim from the earth, and in case of being taken off to keep the secret of it until such a time as they would be able to return again.

Other people would, of course, have to be taken into the secret, and as Drew, with his wealth, was no longer available, some other person with a fortune would have to be induced to join them.

Strange to say, it was the captain who almost despaired when he came to this point, and Jim who seemed easy on the subject.

"If ever we do get to old England again," he said, "the rest will be easy."

On the evening of the second day the captain looked out, and announced a welcome change in the appearance of the sky.

"To-morrow," he said, "will see the beginning of another spell of fine weather, and then we will go to work."

Jim was not sorry to hear it.

Life in a hut is all very well for a time, but the romance of it soon wears off, and young blood inclines to outdoor life, therefore would the charge be welcome.

Neither needed any calling when that morrow came. Before it was fairly light they were up and stirring.

After a wash at a spring adjacent to the hut Jim started with his cooking, it being his turn that morning.

Captain Broadman went out for a stroll to "look over his property," as he humorously observed, "and see that nobody had stolen it in the night."

Jim's heart was light. He sang as he worked, for with the return of the clear sky everything was bright and hopeful.

He had got but half through his work when he heard hurried footsteps outside, and Captain Broadman came dashing into the hut.

The door had a bolt at the bottom, which he drew, and then turned a face curiously white under the tan of his skin towards Jim.

"Stop the cooking," he said; "we have no time to eat just now."

"What is it that troubles you?" asked Jim, anxiously.

"Mawattas — a swarm of them," replied the captain.

The answer was a blow as deadly as that from a hammer, and Jim staggered back half-stunned.

In one moment all the joy and hope of the morning was scattered.

"There's two dozen at least," said the old seaman, hoarsely, "and they haven't seen me as yet. But they are prowling from hut to hut, and will soon be here."

He was no coward, but as brave a man as ever trod the deck of a ship. It was the shock of surprise that unnerved him.

He was walking quietly up and down, not far away from the hut, when he saw a swarthy figure come out of a clump of trees.

He was immediately followed by a dozen more, and all were armed in the crude fashion of their tribe.

As they went straight to a hut near the grove the captain saw they were having a prowl around, probably to see if there were any forgotten or overlooked fragments they could pick up; but whatever mission they might be on it was quite certain they would soon be there.

"We must fight them with fair weapons first," he said to Jim—"the rifle and the revolver. As a last resource I must risk a dynamite cartridge or two."

"Don't forget what is stored there," said Jim, pointing to the other part of the hut.

"I forget nothing," he replied. "It will be better that all should go, and us with it, rather than we should fall into the hands of these fiends. Jim, Jim, I haven't told you before, but let it nerve your arm now—the Mawattas always eat their victims ALIVE!"

"While I have life," returned Jim, with set teeth, "they won't take *me*."

The door did not fit so close as it might do. There were chinks through which a view of the outside was obtainable. Captain Broadman put his eyes to one of them and reported like a man aloft.

"Here they are coming along.   Teyuhetheet

—one looks curiously at the smoke—they are talking. Here they come, like fiends.   Jim, look to the door ; I must guard the window."

The shutter had been taken down to let in the light, and it was lying away on the other side of their habitation.

Before the old seaman could pick it up and replace it a series of yells were heard, and the savages threw themselves against the door.

At the same moment two or three faces appeared at the window.

"Let fly ! my lad," cried the old seaman, as he sent a shot through the window.

But Jim reserved his fire until he saw the top of the door bending in with the pressure, and then he fired into the thick of a knot of savages howling outside.

The effect of the discharge was to drive them back yelling, leaving two dead men behind them.

The door sprung to again, and the virtual captives took breath.

"So far all's well," said the captain, "but they won't give us up.   They are tenacious, and will come again and again, until they get at us.   Hungry wolves are more likely to be scared than they are."

"We ought to have pierced the hut for shooting," said Jim.

"A good thought, my lad," replied the captain, "but rather late."

He had by this time picked up the wooden shutter, and soon succeeded in fixing and bolting it.

As the savages had no firearms they could only now attack by the door.

The howling outside had ceased, and a peep

through one of the cracks showed that the savages were no longer in sight.

"We've scared them away," said Jim.

"Out of sight only," answered the captain; "they won't leave us. They are holding a council of war, and the next thing they will try is FIRE."

"Do you mean they will burn us out?"

"Yes, my lad—it's an old savage dodge. Stop a moment; I see them all lying down in a cluster of bushes. Now, if I durst do it."

He stood still with a musing air, as a man who is debating the results of a risky venture might do.

"Is it anything that I can perform?" asked Jim.

"It's simple but risky," said the old seaman. "I was thinking that if one of us rushed out and cast a dynamite cartridge into the thick of 'em we might perhaps settle the lot. There's some in the stores that would blow fifty men away."

"Give me one," replied Jim; "I'll do it."

"It wants smartness," urged the captain, "for if you miss it's certain death. They only want two seconds to jump up and throw their spears. They are squatting on their haunches pow-wowing now."

"I tell you I will do it," said Jim.

"As you like, my lad," replied the old seaman; "and if they kill you I'll throw open the door, dash in among the stores, and, when they are all in, I'll send up the hut, themselves, and— There, it's not the end of the venture I looked for, but it will be better than the end they intend for us."

He laid down his rifle and walked slowly to the store-room, bidding Jim keep watch outside.

After an absence of a few minutes he came

back with a small box, which he opened. Lodged
securely in wadding was a bomb with cap nipples
sticking out in various directions like the thorns of
a prickly pear.

The percussion caps were in a separate piece of
paper.

"Once thrown there is no chance of its not going
off," he said.

With great care he took out the caps one by one,
placed them carefully on the nipples, and pressed
them gently home.

"It was Drew himself who made this stuff," he said,
"from a recipe of his own.   He told me that old-
fashioned dynamite is a fool to it. Don't drop it, my
lad, for Heaven's sake !"

"Give it to me," said Jim, with a face as quiet as
if he were asking for an ordinary stone to throw at a
foe.

The old seaman gave it to him and walked up to
the door.

"The moment I open," he said, "rush out, and
let 'em have it in the thick of 'em.   As you throw
it fall, for it will send big stones flying about like
feathers."

Jim nodded by way of reply, and waited for the
door to be opened.

The bolt was drawn by the captain so as to make
no noise, and Jim dashed out.

Three long bounds he took, then, seeing a group
of dark forms squatting among the bushes, he cast
the bomb and dropped upon his face.

CHAPTER XXI.

THE EFFECT OF THE EXPLOSION—BURYING THE DEAD—WORKING A RICH VEIN.

APTAIN BROADMAN felt the shock so far as to be blown half way across the hut by the current of air that rushed into it, but he received no material injury.

Nor did the contents of the inner store-room of the hut receive any damage beyond a loose board having been dislodged from its position in the partition.

Outside the hut serious work had been done, for of all the Mawatta men who had been gathered there in council not one had escaped with life.

Some had been simply blown to pieces, others had died quickly from big, gaping wounds, and a few had perished from injuries scarcely perceptible to the eye.

In the latter case minute particles of metal had been driven into some vital portion of their frame and slain them.

Jim was half buried in the loose earth that first rose in the air and then fell around, but he had escaped serious hurt.

On rising he saw before him a place scooped out in the earth, big enough and deep enough to lay the foundation of a good-sized house.

Slowly the captain emerged from the hut, and stood by the side of his young friend, for a few moments regarding the scene.

"Truly," he said at last, as he drew a deep

breath, "Norman Drew has found a new power. Why, dynamite is child's play to it."

They had no reason to doubt that all their enemies had perished, for Jim climbed a tree and scanned the country for fugitives, but none could be seen.

Assured of being for the present unmolested, he descended, and with the aid of the captain performed the uncongenial task of burying the dead.

Their grave was already prepared by the explosion, and in the hollow the remains of the Mawattas were laid.

With all speed the two men covered them with the loose sand-soil, and afterwards went in search of their canoes.

They found them upon the beach, drawn up high and dry, and left unguarded. A spot was selected, handy for the purposes of transportation, where the canoes were hidden in some stunted undergrowth between the wood and the shore.

"So far all is well," said the captain, "but, my lad, our good luck won't last for ever. If another body of Mawattas come they may turn the tables upon us. I am afraid we can do little here *alone*."

It was his first admission that failure lay like a shadow upon him, but instead of further depressing Jim it had the contrary effect.

"We will do all we can," he said, "and bear the rest. I do not despise the means of making money, although I do not think we ought to give our whole souls to it."

"No, but wealth is good," replied the captain, sententiously; "it is the medium by which great communities exist. Half the products of the world would lie unheeded if there was no money."

Jim assented to this, and at once the task of

working the mineral wealth around them was begun.

Metal of some sort was to be found everywhere at a certain depth in the earth, but only the richer kinds were to be worked.

After testing the ground here and there they came upon a vein of tin, one of the most valuable of minerals, and at once set to work.

Having traced it on its course in the direction of the sea—it ran exactly as if at one time a rivulet of liquid tin had run down to the deep—the ground being dry, the metal was drilled here and there for blasting.

Into the hollows thus made cartridges were inserted and fired with slow matches, Jim and the captain taking care to give the place of action a very wide berth.

In this way they were engaged for several days, turning out a mass of ore worth hundreds of pounds.

It was ripped and rent into many fantastic forms, but that was nothing. By and bye, at their leisure, they could reduce it into bar form with the aid of the furnace erected in the hut, originally intended for a smelting-house.

Thus a whole fortnight was employed, and they saw no signs of a foe. Little by little their watchfulness relaxed, and at last one morning the customary precaution of climbing the "look-out" tree was neglected.

And it so chanced that on that day a foe more dangerous than the Mawattas was drawing very nigh.

Strange to say, Captain Broadman that morning referred to the good a watch-dog would be, and expressed regret at having slain the hound that came with the first Mawatta.

"It was some ship's dog," he said, "and had probably been picked up from a wreck."

"The breed is of little use," returned Jim, "except for hunting deer. We kept them at home—"

He stopped short, and, picking up his spade ready for work, began to whistle.

The captain slightly knitted his brows, but he let it pass. When anyone was indisposed to confide in him he was not going to ask for their confidence.

While they laboured that day a ship was approaching the island on the accessible side—a trader blown out of her course by the recent storm, and in need of water.

She dropped her anchor about two miles from the shore, and three times that distance from the two toilers. A boat was lowered, some empty casks put into her, and, with a crew of six men, it was rowed ashore.

The hope of finding water easily was not gratified, for the boat had landed at a spot where springs were scarce.

Convinced that it was an uninhabited island, the men were allowed to disperse, being instructed, however, to hunt for the water in couples.

Two of them paired off, a Frenchman and an Englishman—a couple of ill-looking scoundrels—the latter carrying an axe, as a handy weapon against any attack o savage men or wild beasts.

By chance they took the direction of the spot occupied by Jim and the captain, and ere long had discovered the nearest hut.

They knew at once that, crude as it was as a

a building, it was the work of civilised hands, and they were about to boldly enter it when the arm of the Frenchman was seized by his companion.

"Save my bones! Look there," hissed the Englishman.

The Frenchman looked, and saw two men approaching, bearing something heavy between them.

"Why it's ze boy and ze captain," hissed the Frenchman.

"It is—I thought I was dreaming," replied the Englishman, "but if you see 'em as well it's all right. By a bit o' luck we've come right on 'em again."

The speakers were Dan Ricketts and Morbeau.

CHAPTER XXII.

THE RUFFIANS ON THE ISLE—THEY ARRANGE A PLAN TO STAY—THE FURY GOES AWAY.

 ES, the two villains had escaped a richly-deserved fate—being picked up by the Fury—a trader owned by its captain, a man who sailed anywhere and everywhere, if there was a chance of business being done.

Sometimes he kept to civilised parts, at other times he made for distant islands, and took in a cargo of cocoa-nuts or products of savage industry. He was not at all particular. So it chanced that he dropped upon the lone isle, where Dan Ricketts and Morbeau had been left, and picked them up.

Of course they told him a pitiful story about a wreck, of which they were the sole survivors, having swum ashore in a storm, and the easy-going captain of the Fury accepted it as the truth.

His crew being short, he enrolled them, and now they were brought by chance, or what you will, into the neighbourhood of the men who had suffered so much by their villainy.

Hiding themselves behind some bushes, they saw the old captain and Jim enter the hut hard by and leave their burden there.

On coming out again they were seen to return to a spot where spades and other digging tools were lying about. What was it that they had left in the hut?

As soon as it was safe to leave their hiding-places Dan Ricketts and Morbeau crept up to the hut. The door stood ajar, and they stole in.

Upon the floor, piled up, were heaps of metal, which, in the eyes of Dan Ricketts, appeared to be silver.

Morbeau was also of the same opinion. Anyway, it was valuable, and before them was a treasure worth several thousand pounds.

"Fancy the crafty old thief having got here!" said Dan Ricketts; "and it was the place he was bound for, you bet. Now, Morbeau, have you got a heart in you?"

"I think so," replied the Frenchman.

"If you have," said Ricketts, "stand by me to work out a notion of mine. Here are these two— the only two—on this 'ere island."

"But who build ze hut?" asked Morbeau.

"Never mind that. We'll work it out presently. I can see these two warmints have got it all in their own hands.   Now, why shouldn't you and me get it into ours ?"

" Ze captain of ze Fury vill miss us."

"Miss and leave us," said Ricketts. "If we stick where we are the other chaps will find water some-where, and, having waited for us, will go away. I don't think he is particularly fond of us."

Morbeau laughed as he replied—

"*Sacre !* No. He looks at us out of ze corner of his eye. As you vill. I am vith you."

"Let us get away from here—skulk around inland, where we can see what the Fury does, and then, as soon as she leaves, arrange our plans."

"Good," said the Frenchman.

Dan Ricketts was not mistaken about the opinion the captain of the Fury had of him. He had never liked the addition to the crew, and of late had marked them down as dangerous fellows.

Whatever gratitude the two hang-dog ruffians had felt at first had long evaporated, and they had at times shown a spirit of insubordination.

Therefore, when they did not return—the other men having found water—he waited for them for an hour or two and then set sail, leaving them to their fate.

"They won't starve," was his mental comment. "and they won't perish with cold, while the world will not miss them much. Therefore let them be. Anyway, they are no worse off than when I found them."

So the Fury came and unwittingly deposited these evil ruffians, who had a good chance of carrying out their nefarious designs.

How they succeeded or failed we now propose to tell.

CHAPTER XXIII.

THE DISCOVERY OF THE BOX—CONTENTS OF A DIARY—DAN RICKETTS ON THE WAR TRAIL.

EING in blissful ignorance of the coming and going of the Fury, and of the presence of foes upon the island, Jim and the captain pursued their labours, blasting the vein of metal by degrees, and storing up the jagged pieces rent asunder.

On the night of the arrival of Dan Ricketts and Morbeau, Jim made a discovery in the hut. Observing that the beaten earth which served as a floor had the appearance of having been disturbed within a measurable space of time, he called the attention of the captain to it, and the conclusion they arrived at was that something was concealed beneath.

A few blows with a pick and a turn or two with a spade revealed the fact that a box had been buried there. Having dug it up, the old captain recognised it as having been the property of Norman Drew, the scientist.

"I wonder why it was buried there?" he mused, as he lifted it from its resting-place.

"Is it locked?" asked Jim.

The captain tried the lid, and found it was

WITH SNAKE-LIKE MOVEMENTS THE FIGURE OF DAN RICKETTS EMERGED FROM THE WOOD.

unfastened. Opening the box, he saw a quantity of papers and memorandum-books within.

"We'll have a look at these outside after supper," said Captain Broadman.

Of late, the nights being warm, they had been accustomed to spend an hour outside before going to bed, lying on the ground and looking at the stars while they talked.

Sometimes they had a bit of a fire "for company," and on this occasion they had it for use.

It would serve as a lamp to read the papers by.

After a quiet supper and a smoke they carried out the box, and Jim, having gathered together and lighted the materials for a fire, they sat down to read.

Captain Broadman took out the first paper and read the following inscription upon it—

"*To whosoever may find this box the records of a disastrous expedition are dedicated.*"

"I wonder how he hoped the box would be found?" asked Jim.

"There's an arrow, point downwards, scratched on the timber inside," replied the captain. "I noticed it to night for the first time."

"Shall I read what is inside?" asked Jim. "My sight is better than yours."

"Aye! do, my lad."

Jim took the paper, opened it, and read the following written in a clear, bold hand :—

"*I write this at a moment of great peril, when all but myself are boxed up in Watts' hut, without arms or ammunition, and I am alone within these wooden walls. Death or a miserable captivity is certain for us all.*

been done since our dear friend Captain Broadman went back to England to procure necessary materials for our work.

"Let it be known at home what has become of us, and if our bodies are not found it may be assumed that we have simply been made captives. In that case I rely upon the world-famed liberality of our countrymen to send out an expedition in search of us. If living we may most likely be found on the Mawatta Island."

"Jim," cried the captain, striking the ground with his clenched fist, "we haven't found a body here."

"No," assented Jim, thoughtfully.

"Then it stands to reason that they are alive."

Jim was about to make a hopeful response when a slight sound attracted his attention. It was just as if some animal was stealing about in the wood hard by.

He cast his eyes in that direction, and the captain, observing the pause, asked him what he saw.

"Nothing," answered Jim; "but I fancied I heard something."

They sat quite still for a time, but the sound was not repeated, and the captain said it was nothing more than some insect chirping in the undergrowth.

Diving his hand in the box, he brought out some papers, and, selecting one, saw that it was a list of researches, with the results, which had been made on the island since he went away.

This promised to be interesting, but it could wait, and the old seaman placed it in his pocket. A number of sheets, stitched together, and marked "Rough Diary," next came to hand.

It was not yet dark by any means. The sun was dipping, and in a few minutes night would be there, so the captain passed the diary over to Jim.

"Skim it through, my lad," he said; "pick out the striking bits."

Jim unfolded the paper, bent it back so as to get it tolerably flat, and glancing over the first page read out—

"June 19th.—Have had a week's rain, and we intended, as the change had come, to begin work to-day, but Watts was taken ill early in the morning. It was nothing serious, however, for at night the feverish symptoms had passed away. He fancied it arose from his having tested the quality of a strange fruit—not unlike the grape—which he found in the wood.

"June 20th.—At work all day. See record of researches.

"June 21, 2, 3, 4, 5th.—Ditto.

"June 26th.—Canoes discovered out at sea and approaching the island. Quite a number of them. Must be bringing two hundred savages at least.

"June 27th.—Savages did not land. After coming within a mile of land they sheered off in a western direction. General joy. Work resumed.

"28th.—Work all day. At night glare of fire in a distant part of the island. I went out scouting to see who ignited it. Discovered a horde of cannibals on the west coast feasting on enemies they had captured. Made an effort to return home, but lost my way.

"29th.—After wandering all night—lost in the wood, owing to a haze hiding the stars—came in sight of the old place, and found cannibals there before me, surrounding Watts' hut. Managed to slip unseen into the workshop, and lay close, to watch what was going on. Seeing cannibals opposite, barricaded the door."

Then followed the record of two days' siege—

"The savages, having no arms but spears, bows, and arrows, could not force the door. Indeed, they gave up their whole time, or nearly so, in assaulting the building which contained the rest of the men."

"Norman Drew must have been occupying some of his time in preparing a hiding-place for the box," the captain here interposed.

The final record was very brief, but pregnant with disaster.

"Have no water—am burning with thirst; must soon yield. Death is preferable to the agonies I endure in this heated place. There are signs of the others yielding also. The door of Watts' hut has been opened once, as if they were about to rush forth. But it was closed again. As they have no water, like my unfortunate self, they must soon give in."

While these portentous entries in the diary were being read the figure of Dan Ricketts, with snake-like movements, had been emerging from the wood. He carried an axe in his hand, and his eyes glittered with the baleful look of a murderer.

Could he but strike the captain down, Morbeau, crouching tiger-like in the wood, was ready to spring out upon Jim, who betrayed no signs of having arms about him.

But Jim had now become habituated to carrying a revolver with him, and he had one ready to hand in the breast of his shirt.

Still, he had as yet no suspicion of the vicinity of

his old foe, who was careful to keep the somewhat bulky body of the captain between them.

Moreover, the deepening gloom was in his favour, and the first part of his plot to destroy would have been successful but for one of those slips which often occur to mar an evil design.

In crawling along the ground he put his hand upon a small, ant-like insect, which promptly stung him.

As a bite it was not very severe. It was the surprise that drew a short, sharp exclamation of anger from Ricketts.

Jim and the captain leapt up just in time to see the ruffian vanish in the woods. The old seaman was not certain of his identity, but Jim knew him.

"It's Ricketts!" he cried.

"My lad," replied the captain, "it isn't possible."

They plunged into the wood side by side, but could see nobody. Both the would-be murderer and his companion had vanished.

In the growing gloom it would be more than useless to attempt pursuit. No trail of man or beast could have been followed, and it was with a sense of insecurity they returned to open ground.

"Gather up the papers," said the captain, "while I quench every spark of fire. If by any chance that black-hearted villain is here he may not have the means of lighting one, and that's a weapon less.

"He had an axe," replied Jim, grimly, "and, as far as I could see, he meant to use it too. What's to be done? We can't work with freedom if he's prowling around."

"Was he alone?"

"As far as I could see."

"He may or may not be," said the old seaman, musingly. "Now I've got a little scheme just come into my head, which I think will circumvent him and others, if there be such with him, so come inside and we'll bar the door and sit down and talk it over."

He was busy while speaking in treading out the fire.

Not a single spark did he leave to be utilised by the enemy. This much done for their safety, they adjourned to the hut, bolted the door, fastened up the window, and indulged in the rare luxury of lighting a lamp.

"Now for our trunks of clothes," said the captain.

"Our clothes?" exclaimed Jim, opening his eyes.

"Yes, our clothes," repeated the captain, "and then I'll show you a little game that will, I believe, circumvent Dan Ricketts, cunning as he is. Give me mine first."

CHAPTER XXIV.

THE CAPTAIN'S PLAN—TAKEN IN BY DUMMIES.

Y plan," said the captain, "is dummies. We'll stuff two suits of clothes and put 'em out as if they were talking together, and that 'ere fellow will be sure to come round again. But we will wait a day or so, as he'll hold off for a time."

It was late before they went to bed, probably about two in the morning. They had progressed well with their labours, and two very fair imitations of the human face and figure had been nearly completed.

Jim, who was a bit of an artist, moulded the

faces with wet clay, which he dug up from the beaten floor, using pieces of charcoal for the eyes.

The old captain said they were "more natural than life," which may be considered to be a very glowing compliment a little outside fact, but Jim was moderately satisfied they would deceive ordinary eyes in the twilight a few yards away.

The next day they spent within easy distance of the hut, having their eyes on the watch and their arms ready for use.

Dan Ricketts, as the captain expected, did not reappear.

During the night the dummies were completed, and just before dawn two holes were pierced in the wall of their abode, so as to enable a rifle to bear upon the spot of their old camp fire.

Some wood was got together and three cross sticks set over it, with a pot suspended therefrom. The figure bearing a resemblance to the captain was laid in a reclining attitude, and that like Jim in the position of a man watching the cooking.

The fire was then lighted, and the pair hurriedly retreated to the hut, where they loaded their rifles and prepared for action.

"He's bound to have another go at us," said the captain, "especially as he knows his life aint safe here—provided, of course, it is Ricketts."

"It was the scoundrel. I am sure of it."

Half an hour's watching somewhat tired them, for it is weary work waiting for anything the coming of which is not at all certain ; but at last they were rewarded, and the dummy plan proved to be an unqualified success.

This time not only Ricketts, but Morbeau, were seen stealing down from bush to bush, each armed with an axe—two desperate men, bent upon a daring rush for success.

The astonishment of the captain was sufficient to make him gasp.

" Why, they are both here !" he said.

" And alone," returned Jim, " or they would not attack us without assistance."

The scoundrels were just clear of the wood, lying on the flat of their stomachs, with their eyes fixed upon the two still figures.

" Captain," said Jim, suddenly, " they are beginning to suspect our little game. You take Morbeau, and I'll let fly at Ricketts. Quick !"

Rapidly both took aim. The captain was an expert with the rifle, and Jim, by practice, was a pretty fair shot.

Each covered his man and pulled the trigger.

Ricketts had indeed suspected something. The unnatural stillness of the dummies would, have soon awakened suspicion in any ordinary mind, and he was as cunning as a fox.

He had just given a hasty word of warning to Morbeau, and both were rising to their feet, with the object of scuttling away, when the rifles sent forth their deadly missiles to do as good work as ever powder and lead did in this world.

Morbeau threw out his arms convulsively, and fell upon his side—dead.

Ricketts uttered a piercing cry, clapped a hand to his heart, made one staggering effort to retreat, and then sunk upon his knees.

" Got 'em !" cried the captain, exultingly.

Opening the door he rushed out, followed by Jim, each with a revolver in his hand; but they had no need to use either weapon upon the fallen men.

Morbeau, as stated, was dead, and Ricketts was dying.

The axe he carried had fallen from his hand, and when he saw the captain and Jim approaching the effort he made to pick it up again was feeble and futile.

He was a doomed man, and he knew it, while the mortification he felt was harder to bear than the pains and deadly weakness he felt from the wound in his side.

" You needn't shoot, captain," he gasped ; " I'm a goner."

" Ricketts," said the captain. " you've brought your fate upon yourself. Had you been an honest man there would have been a fortune for you. I meant kindly by you all."

" Took in by dummies at the last," muttered Ricketts ; "that's what riles me—took in by dummies ! Whose idea was it—that young warmint's ?"

" It doesn't matter who it was," said the captain ; "it was good enough for you. Don't waste your time in reviling us—think of your approaching end."

" I can't think of nothing," moaned Ricketts, " but what's HERE. To be so nigh getting hold of it, and then to be—took in by dummies."

" How came you here?" asked Captain Broadman, kneeling down beside him. " Was it chance?"

" Yes—chance, that's all—beastly chance. But I felt for a long time that I'd got to die by the hand of one of you. Who did it—who fired at me? I want to curse him."

" Don't do that," observed the old seaman, gravely; " it won't hurt him or help you."

"Oh! it won't hurt *him*," said Ricketts, with an evil flash in his eyes. "So the young 'un did it. I said he was agin me when we started in the Lapwing, and I wanted to chuck him overboard afore we'd been two days at sea. But the other fools wouldn't hear of it—they said it would raise suspicion. And then that 'ere craft must come and take us off and bring me here to him—the luck of it—the luck of it."

He lay back gasping for a few moments, and then made another effort to speak. His words now came slowly, and were scarcely audible.

No effort was made to help him, for the captain saw it was all over with him.

"But for *him*," muttered Ricketts, "I'd ha' been rich, and you might be lying here 'stead o' me. The luck of it! And for me—to—to—be took in—by—DUMMIES!"

He clenched his hands and made a feeble, despairing attempt to rise, with the indefinite object of doing Jim an injury, and then fell back—arms and legs stretched out and his distorted face raised up to the morning light—dead.

CHAPTER XXV.

PREPARING FOR DEFENCE—JIM TELLS HIS STORY TO THE CAPTAIN.

N hour later Ricketts and Morbeau were buried by Jim and the captain.

"We'll give 'em that grace," said the latter; "every murderer has it in the prisons at home."

As there was deeper soil near the wood the grave for two was dug there, and the spot marked with a rough wooden cross.

"They're gone," said the captain, "and we'll say no more about them. We won't be their judges after death."

"You are right, captain," replied Jim; "but their end shows what fools men are when they take to crooked ways. What have they gained by the ghastly crimes they committed on board the Lapwing and all that they have done since?"

"Nothing," replied the captain, "but they have lost much."

The need of ever being on the defensive, although no enemy might be in sight, was now evident to both, and before proceeding with their ordinary labour means for protecting themselves in case of being attacked were taken in hand.

The hut was pierced for rifle-shooting on every side, and quite a little armoury of weapons with ammunition kept ready for use.

The chief fear of the captain was the arriving of a further contingent of the Mawatta people.

He argued that those who had already met with death upon the island would be missed and sought for by the others.

As a people the Mawattas were as revengeful as the Corsicans, and carried out their vengeance without stint.

It afforded them the joy of retaliation and gratified their lust for blood.

" Sooner or later, my lad," said the captain, " we shall have a swarm of 'em here, and we must be prepared."

Having got the hut ready for defence, the next thing was to put together the field-piece which has been previously referred to.

A skilled mechanic would have been of good service here, but both the captain and Jim had the knack of turning their hands to almost anything, and piece by piece they got it together, and planted it on the open ground midway between the two huts.

" Before using," said the captain, " it will have to be tested, in case we haven't got it as it ought to be. That'll be a ticklish job—a case of a slow match and a sharp run."

Jim laughingly admitted the necessity of it, as the bursting of a gun when firing at a foe might be a disaster not easily remedied.

So the gun was loaded with a double charge of powder, rammed home tight enough to fully test its firing qualities, and a small slow-match fitted to the touch-hole

" You get away, captain," said Jim, " and I'll fire it. I can run twice as fast as you."

The old seaman retreated to a safe distance, and

Jim, with great deliberation, lighted the match and trotted off in the same direction.

Ere he had covered half the ground between them the gun went off with a boom that echoed all over the island and far away to sea.

"Stood it like a rock," cried the captain, exultingly; "she's a beauty. We'll begin to build a bit of a shelter over her to-morrow—just sufficient to keep off the rain when it comes. Something that can be thrown down when we go into action."

"It wouldn't do to have it inside the hut, I suppose?" said Jim, doubtfully.

"No, my lad," replied the captain; "we must keep her well in the open, or the shock of the discharge might start the dynamite, and then where would we be?"

At present there was no sign of a coming storm, and the gun was left where it was until the morrow.

As the work of the day had been rather stiff the two men retired early, but they did not go to sleep.

Both, for some reason, were very wakeful, and presently Jim was heard to speak.

"Captain," he said, "shall I tell you my story? There isn't much in it to amuse you or for me to be proud of, but I feel you ought to know it, and I would rather tell it in the dark."

"If there's any shame in it," replied the captain, quietly, "don't let me know of it. I've got a good opinion of you now, and I want to keep it."

"It isn't exactly shame," returned Jim, "but the fact is I haven't been a good son—I'm a runaway from home."

"That I've always reckoned," said the captain.

"And I'm not a swell," continued Jim. "My father was a farmer."

"All honour to him," rejoined the old seaman; "he is better than a rich idler."

"I am an only son," said Jim, after a pause, "and of course was spoilt a bit. My father was once a thriving man. His farm at one time paid well, and I was sent to a good school at an early age. When about thirteen I was removed to the grammar school in an adjoining town, and it was there I got hold of notions that raised me up above corn-growing and cow-keeping."

"I wonder what fool did that for you?" growled the captain.

"Lots of fools playing on a fool," answered Jim. "Anyway, the mischief was done. When my father wanted me to come home and assist him, for times were not so good as they were, I grumbled, and said I would rather have some business that would take me abroad and make me rich. I'd got an idea of trading with ships all over the globe, and that sort of thing. It never occurred to me that I should want no end of capital to do it."

"And make a mess of it after all," said the captain, with a chuckle.

"Just so," assented Jim. "I see it now. Well, I did go home to the farm, but with my grammar-school notions in my head I was more than useless there. I made the old people uncomfortable, there's no doubt about that, and I was miserable myself. At last I made up my mind to run away to London, as being the nearest place where I could see some shipping and learn something about the sea. I was eighteen then, and really greener than I ought to have been, because—"

"You had never been vicious," interposed the captain. "Just so—go on."

"Well, I got to London," resumed Jim, "but I had no opportunity to hang about and study shipping, for some rascal picked my pocket of my purse, and the strike was on, so, hearing you wanted men, I thought I would become a sailor and chance the rest. You see, I felt I couldn't go sneaking back almost as soon as I started, and—and that's the story."

"I'm sorry for your father and mother," said the captain, after a pause of some duration. "They must be grieving about you."

"I meant to write to them from the first port I touched at," replied Jim, "but I didn't think matters would turn out as they did."

"They never do come about as we lay 'em out," observed the captain, sententiously.

"What grieves me is that when I go back—if ever I do get back—I may find the old people GONE."

"Let's hope it won't be so bad as that," said the captain. "As for getting back, *we're* going one day —I feel it. I'm glad, my lad, you have told me your story, and I can understand that a lad of your mettle felt a bit shy in coming out with it; but there's nothing in it to be ashamed of, although there's a little to regret. Keep up a stout heart and all will be well by and bye. Good-night, my lad."

"Good-night, captain."

Somehow the story had a soothing effect upon them both, and a few minutes later they were quietly sleeping.

CHAPTER XXVI.

THE MAWATTAS' RETURN—DESPERATE FIGHTING.

SAGACIOUS humourist —Artemus Ward, to wit —once gave a good piece of advice to prophets in general, and that was, "Never to prophecy unless you know."

It is a good maxim, but, even if you don't know, it occasionally happens that you may prophecy right.

Thus it was with good old Captain Broadman and the Mawattas.

He prophesied their coming, and they came promptly.

It was only the day after the gun had been tested that Jim, having ascended the look-out, saw a number of canoes approaching the island. He descended and reported to the captain, who, in turn, climbed up half-way, and with the aid of his glass got a good view of the approaching party.

"Mawattas," was his report, as soon as he had returned to *terra firma*. "Jim, we must load the gun and be prepared to give 'em a hot reception."

To do justice to the occasion he went indoors and put on his best coat, and armed himself with a cutlass.

Thus accoutred he felt ready for the encounter which he was sure would take place.

Jim had meanwhile loaded the gun with a full charge of powder, and instead of the usual projectile had rammed home a number of bullets and pieces of iron, which would not fail to create havoc among an advancing body of men.

"They are fully armed," said the captain, "and all on the war-path. It is as I said; they have come out to find their friends—to rescue them if alive and if dead to avenge them. Now, Jim, listen to me."

"I'm all attention," said Jim.

"We must keep an eye on the Mawattas and make sure of their line of advance towards us. They may come direct or not—most likely direct, as we have left a pretty clear trail from the beach to this spot."

"Are they good at a trail?" asked Jim.

"Bloodhounds, I should say," replied the captain. "When I was off their island years ago we used to see 'em on the trail of an animal just like hounds, but it wasn't easy to tell whether they were going by sight or scent—perhaps a little of each."

Jim now volunteered to ascend the tree again, and the captain bade him be careful, so as not to show any of his body. The old seaman had an idea that the Mawattas, in addition to their other gifts, had the clear, far-reaching sight of the vulture.

So Jim went up cautiously, keeping close to the trunk and as much as possible behind it.

The canoes were by this time pretty close to the beach, and he counted eighteen in all.

The number of occupants varied from six to a dozen, and in the bow of each one a man was standing up closely scanning the shore.

On his reaching the ground again and announcing the near vicinity of the foe, the gun was put about so that its muzzle pointed, as near as they could guess, towards the point of approach.

They could not make sure of the exact direction, but they could be fairly acurate, so that at the last moment very little movement would enable them to have the weapon correctly aimed.

Then they stood still and waited.

Not a sound was heard of the approaching foe.

The canoes were very light, and would ground upon the beach without making much noise, if, indeed, they were near enough to be heard.

But the landing-place was at least a mile away, and only a sound of some magnitude could have reached the ears of Jim and his companion.

"Crafty, cruel, and *dumb*, generally," said the captain, softly. "When they see us they will make their rush, and we sha'n't have much time for aiming."

"I've got the muzzle at the proper level," said Jim; "it is only a question of direction—you may leave that to me.

"All right, my lad."

After that they stood still and waited, neither speaking.

If the Mawattas had struck the trail they would soon be upon them, but if they had not there might be a delay of hours, or even a day and night.

But sooner or later they would come.

Jim, in his heart, wished they would come at once.

He had the natural impatience of youth, and wanted to get the inevitable over—the more so as he had the reliance of bravery, and felt almost certain victory would be on his side.

A quarter of an hour later and the Mawattas appeared.

They came bounding out of the wood, running with their heads down and their eyes fixed on the trail, exactly as the old captain had described them, like hounds in full pursuit.

Captain Broadman drew his sword and loosened the revolvers in his belt. Jim quietly swung the gun round on the line of the advancing savages.

A cry from one of the foremost was heard, and in a moment all were erect.

They saw their foes ahead, and a yelping cry, which made them appear more like hounds than ever, leaped in wild chorus from their throats.

Jim stooped and ran his eye along the gun.

It appeared to be sighted correctly.

It was fired in the old-fashioned way—by drawing a fuse across the touch-hole.

Jim paused a moment with a very creditable hesitation, arising from a dislike of slaughter; but it was a case of their lives or his, and he applied the match.

The gun belched forth its fire with a dreadful roar, and a line of iron missiles struck the savage horde well in the centre.

A score or so were literally cut up, but many remained unhurt.

The range was a short one, and the shot did not spread sufficiently to put the greater part of the band *hors de combat*.

Instead of destroying it utterly, the party of savages was cut in two.

Those unhurt were staggered and alarmed, but they did not flee.

It was more than probable that they had heard the roar of a big gun before. Be that as it may, they quickly rallied, and came charging on.

"To the hut!" cried the captain.

It would have been madness to stay and face so

many, so Jim and the captain retreated quickly, and got under cover ere the savages could get near enough to throw their spears.

Closing the door, the old seaman quickly barricaded it, and then gave the word for the rifles to be used.

Looking out through one of the loopholes cut for firing, he saw the savages gathered near the gun, regarding it apprehensively, as if they feared it would turn its mouth to them and "speak thunder again."

But seeing it did not stir they made a sudden pounce upon it, and, laying hold of the wheels, tilted it up and turned it over upon its side.

Having performed this feat they began to dance with joy.

"Give 'em pepper, Jim," said the captain, between his teeth.

Two rifles belched out their fire, and two of the dancers fell to rise no more.

This fresh surprise scattered the savages in every direction, but the scare was soon over.

Instead of retreating out of sight they bore down upon one who appeared to be their leader, and gathered around him.

As they were about three hundred yards away the rifles had to be sighted to shoot so far correctly, and while doing this the chief of the savages was indulging in a speech of some sort, gesticulating violently.

"Jim," said Captain Broadman, "that fellow has to be brought down. Try your luck with him."

Jim, nothing loth, for his blood was up, thrust out the muzzle of his rifle and took careful aim.

The savage was not easy to hit, for he moved about rapidly for awhile. At last he stood quite

still, to give full effect to the concluding words of
his speech, whatever they were.

This was Jim's opportunity, and taking careful
aim he fired.

With a howl the savage clapped his hand to his
thigh, made an effort to run, and fell to the ground,
where he lay writhing and kicking about with his
uninjured limb.

His followers spread themselves out and stared
hard at their fallen chief.

Presently he made an attempt to rise, but only to
fall again and renew his kicking.

Then his men seemed to get hold of the notion
that their leader was done for.

Birds and beasts and even insects slay the injured
of their kind, and the instinct to do so appeared to
be in the hearts of the Mawatta.

Nothing was said, and no signal was given so far
as Jim could see, but suddenly, without warning, the
whole body fell upon their leader.

A dozen spears were thrust into his breast, and
the life blood spurted out in streams.

In a moment or two he was dead.

" I'll be hanged," muttered the captain, "if that
doesn't beat everything. Here, let's give 'em another
to operate upon."

He fired his weapon into the thick of the seething
mob, and another savage tumbled to the ground,
where he lay upon his face, clawing the loose soil
with his hands and kicking it up in small clouds with
his feet.

Where he was hit it was impossible to say at that
distance, but he, too, after having been watched for
a few moments by his companions, shared the fate of
his leader.

Having slain him they broke away, and went sweeping and howling towards the wood.

"Let fly at 'em, Jim.   They'll come back again," said the captain.

"Stop!" cried Jim.   "Look there, captain.   Men coming from the wood."

The captain bent down and stared through the opening, when he saw about a dozen men break out and dash madly at the startled savages.

"White men, by Jingo!" he cried.   "Jim, we're saved."

CHAPTER XXVII.

GOOD LUCK TO ALL.

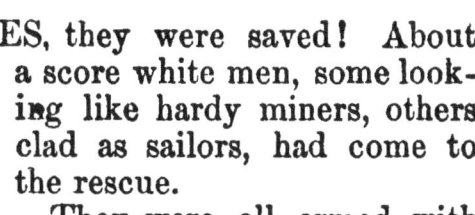

YES, they were saved! About a score white men, some looking like hardy miners, others clad as sailors, had come to the rescue.

They were all armed with rifles or revolvers, and the way they brought down the Mawattas ensured a speedy termination of the lot, save a few who fled away scared.

But before this happened Captain Broadman had come out of his hiding-place, followed by Jim, and was shaking hands with some of the men not in seamen's attire.

One he addressed as Norman Drew and another as Walker, and Jim rightly guessed that the people who had been left upon the island had not been slain after all.

And who who were the sailors with them ? Well, that was explained in the story subsequently told.

The captain's friends, being left without the means of defending themselves, as our readers will remember from the peep they had at the diary of Drew, came out to fight with their fists and stones, but to their astonishment the Mawattas made signs of peace.

The result was they yielded without further fighting, but they were not allowed to retain their freedom.

Being pounced upon by sudden, concerted action, they were bound and carried away to the Mawatta Island, where they had been held captive ever since.

"It seemed that when they took us, captain," said Norman Drew, "they found us pretty well nothing but skin and bone, and their design was to fatten us, like stock, before killing."

"They didn't succeed in putting much flesh on you," said the old captain.

"No, because I knew their object," answered Drew; "and, having a knowledge of herbs, I got hold of some weeds that kept us thin. However, they made up their minds to kill us when the war party returned from an expedition, and that's the party you have just scattered. I ought to tell you that some of 'em went out a short time ago and never returned. It was suspected they had been captured and killed by some of the neighbouring tribes, and that was the reason for the setting out of the second party.

"But while they were away a British cruiser dropped her anchor off the Mawatta Island," continued Drew. "These are some of the men"—introduction here effected with much cordial hand-

THE MUTINY OF THE LAPWING.

shaking. "They sent a party ashore, and we managed to assimilate with them. The result was a considerable reduction in the remnant of the Mawatta tribe and our rescue.

"We asked to be brought over here to see if you had arrived, and when near the island heard the booming of a gun. Then it was feared something was wrong, and the captain of the Iris—that's the name of the gallant craft, and his name is Purday—lent us some arms, and sent us ashore with these good fellows just to see what was up."

Captain Broadman looked uneasy. He had an idea that the arrival of the cruiser would result in the Crown claiming the island. But Drew relieved his mind.

"Purday," he said, "is a good fellow. He says he will mark the island on his chart, and report it as being occupied by a few English settlers, who only desire to be left in peace. As the Iris is homeward bound we can send letters which will ensure the arrival of another vessel for our own use."

"I'll go with her and bring the new ship back," said Captain Broadman, "and take dern good care to get a decent crew this time."

*   *   *   *   *

After lying at anchor for a day or two, to enable an exchange of hospitalities to be made, the Iris set sail for England with Captain Broadman on board.

Acting on the advice of Captain Purday, he was going to apply to the home Government for permission to use the island as the home for a colony, which was sure to be granted him, for who would suspect what a mine of mineral wealth it was?

Neither Captain Purday nor his crew were enlightened in this respect, but they suspected something. Being, however, bound up in their work, they did not trouble their minds about it.

Indeed, they had little opportunity to do so, for almost as soon as the Iris reached home she was sent away to the Mediterranean, to lie off Malta for a year or so, and then on to Cyprus.

．　　．　　．　　．　　．　　．　　．

The rest of the story must be told in brief. The Government granted to Joshua Broadman, master mariner, the right to inhabit and work on the Island of Good Luck—as it was named—*discovered* by Captain Purday and the Iris, and he, the said Joshua Broadman, was appointed to act as interim governor of the aforesaid island for seven years, the governorship to be renewed if desirable.

"What an old fool I was not to think of this at first," growled the captain. "But there, sailors don't know anything of land matters."

．　　．　　．　　．　　．　　．　　．

Jim did not remain on the island seven years, nor, indeed, did the majority of those that first inhabited it.

The discovery of all sorts of valuable metals on this marvellous spot in the ocean enabled them to grow rich speedily.

Instead of sending home all their treasure they despatched a lot of it to San Francisco, where they found a ready market.

Ere long the Yankees discovered where the metal came from, and but for the flag of Old England being hoisted over it they would have filibustered the island and robbed the original owners of their rights.

they dare not, with all their braggadocio, set foot upon it.

. . . .

One day, five years after he left home, Jim Bentley once again set foot upon his native land.

Occasionally he had sent word that he was alive and well, but nothing more did he record— not even to a pretty girl, one Eva Darrell, whom he had loved in a boyish, sweetheartly way before he left England.

No letters came back to him, because he had not given his address, but now that he was the owner of nearly twenty thousand pounds—his share of five years' successful labour on the island— he had come back to see the old folks and Eva.

His intention was to settle down, and, if Eva would have him, to marry her.

During his absence things had gone wrong at the farm. There had been bad times and seasons for the tillers of the soil, and, but for his timely arrival, a few days later would have seen the old place sold up.

With what delight he was received one may guess. An only son returning to parents who love him dearly is one of the best pictures of pure, unalloyed joy to be found on earth.

After the first greetings and congratulations Jim asked for Eva.

He was told that she had developed from a pretty girl into a very handsome woman, and half the young men around were after her.

" But is she engaged to anyone ?" asked Jim.

" Lor! bless you, no, Jim," replied his mother.

you didn't come back then she would wait another ten."

That was all Jim wanted to know, and it practically put everything straight.

He went to see Eva, who was the daughter of a neighbouring farmer, and the meeting gave both the pleasure of finding that absence had strengthened their early love and done wonders in improving their personal appearance.

After this there was nothing to do but marry, which, like wise people, they did without delay.

Jim paid off his father's debts, managed the farm, and with a plentiful supply of capital soon made it pay.

There, if you want to see him, you will find him now, with a charming wife and a couple of youngsters.

The old people reside in a neat little house not far away, and near to Captain Broadman, who has sold his rights in the island for a pretty round sum and has settled in England.

He has a heap of money, which he says will come to Jim by and bye, for if it hadn't been "for the pluck of the lad" his own career would have ended with "THE MUTINY OF THE LAPWING."

THE END.

www.ingramcontent.com/pod-product-compliance
Lightning Source LLC
Chambersburg PA
CBHW080826250626
47160CB00008B/2866